BANG TO BEGIN

by
Jethro Weyman

Reality is Relative.

@WeymanWrites

CHARITY

A loud bang from the basement attracts no more than a few downward glances. What are they doing down there? I'll check later; it's time to begin.

The party's in full swing. Clinking champagne glasses and the click-clack of heels on parquet add percussion to a string quartet playing sonatas on the central podium. The murmurs of my esteemed guests - fellow philanthropists – are punctuated by shrill laughter and the scoffing of exotic delicacies, shipped from every corner of the Earth.

'Welcome,' I say, microphone in hand, 'to the *Wishing Well Gala*. The first of many.'

A sea of expectant eyes swivel towards me. The room falls silent.

'Every penny made this evening will be spent on children who have led a life of pain and suffering. With your help, we can fill the wishing well. We can end their misery.'

Applause from monochrome men and rainbow clad women, glasses held higher than their noses for once. Every sorry soul in the country is here: from inheritance brats to entrepreneurs, nobility to Mafiosi. Not one of them is here for the children. They all want what I have to offer.

Positive publicity.

One can't climb to the top of the ladder without bending a

few rules on the way. A little moral camouflage hides the cracks one leaves in the rungs. No one wants to accuse the people who save the children or the animals. Who wants to criminalise those who donate to local nursing homes or cancer research?

Charitable immunity.

'The auction will begin in fifteen minutes,' I say. 'Please take your seats in the auditorium. Paddles will be handed to you on entry. Thank you.'

A rush of bodies, each wanting the best seats, each wanting to be the first to feast their eyes on my surprises. I climb down the stairs from the lectern, then again, down the stairs to the basement.

Stock check.

Paintings from Russia, from France, from South America. Sculptures from Italy, from Africa and Asia. Signed manuscripts from authors, both dead and alive. Jewellery crafted from the finest stones. Poems and prose of lost civilisations. How much of it is stolen? That is not for me to know. Donations are taken with discretion. The first rule of a successful auction.

Never speculate.

'What was that loud noise earlier?' I ask.

'Nothing, Tobias,' says Diego. 'The wind and some buttered fingers. I've dealt with him.'

'Good,' I say. 'Are we on schedule?'

'We'll be finished by midnight.'

'Perfect.'

*

The auctioneer's gavel hits hard on the first sale. Six figures for an oil painting. A woman in a white robe, alone in a hotel room, spread across ruffled sheets. A pillow scrunched up in balled fists. A shadow beneath the bathroom door. Donated by Don

Stradiotto. A true story, no doubt.

A roman statue for a duke. A diamond brooch for an oil magnate. She collects it immediately, pins it to her mink skin coat as the wishing well floods. Five million by nine o'clock. All for the children. All for their future.

'The first truck's here,' says Diego.

One of three.

'Any issues?' I ask.

'None so far,' he says. 'We'll start preparing the first load straight away.'

'Perfect.'

*

The occasional phone call and blood-drained face of realisation does nothing to spoil the atmosphere. Pride wins auctions, but pride also drains memory. Memory of how rich one really is. One may like something a little too much, perhaps pride conquers reason, causes them to forget how small their bank balance has become, forget they have a family to support, forget they have a family at all - until the damage is already done.

Competitive amnesia.

The second truck rolls in at quarter to eleven. Plenty of time before the main event. One left.

'Please help yourself to canapés and miniatures,' I say to the crowd. 'Stretch your legs. Powder your noses. The auction will continue in ten minutes.'

The last few items are lifted onto the stage, covered with sheets of charmeuse silk. Only the best for such particular clientele.

'Ladies and gentlemen. Welcome to the final hour. We have, of course, saved the best for last.' I gesture towards the disguised articles. 'Beneath these sheets lie some of the finest objects this world has to offer. The most precious of prizes. The most wonderful of wares. Fill the well and take them home. For the children.'

The first veil lifts and the gold detail of a Fabergé egg glistens under the stage lights. The third truck arrives as Diego's broad form rises from the basement.

'The first two loads are prepared,' Diego whispers into my ear. 'This one should bring us up to twenty-one.'

'Perfect.'

*

The last item sells for a ten-figure sum to a lady who owns more islands than the former British Empire. The Indian Sun. A flawless diamond, larger than a baby's head.

I wave goodbye to the journalists and shake the hand of each and every guest that leaves, wishing them well on their onward journeys.

'What a wonderful evening, Tobias,' says Ava Vertu. 'You have no idea how much this means to me, how much it will mean to the children.'

She has an aura. Wherever she walks, it follows, as if the sun has left a little of itself behind just to shelter her from the night. It's obvious why the children love her, why she's so successful in this field of work. I would kiss her on her cheek like I do all the others, but I don't want to taint her, the only pure soul in this room.

'Expect the funds by tomorrow evening, Miss Vertu,' I say. 'Goodnight. Travel well.'

One of the hired security guards closes the door behind her with a click then returns to his mildly-threatening, cross-armed stance, Diego's hissing voice loud enough to hear through his earpiece.

Some of my guests stay, of course, depending where their loyalties lie, grouping closer to the stage and muttering in frantic anticipation.

The auction can't continue without buyers.

'The wishing well may be full, but for you, the select few with exclusive invitations, I present the main event.'

Diego walks slowly onto the stage, a thick rope held firmly in his hands. The first one is small. Skinny legs. Skinny arms. No older than four or five. The blindfold hides her eyes and the gag imprisons her voice. Her steps are clumsy from the drugs, bare feet slapping against hard wood, cheeks slick with tears.

Premium stock.

'First, we have lot 4-7-2. The daughter of Henrietta Larsen,' says the auctioneer, as Diego positions the girl at centre stage. 'Plucked from the Radisson Blu but an hour ago. Still fresh. Shall we start the bidding at one hundred thousand?'

Paddles rise.

Hotel rooms are about as secure as rotting garden sheds, if you know the right people. And I know *all* of the right people. I wonder if Ms Larsen's au pair has woken up yet, or if her mink skin coat has survived the rain.

It wasn't a lie when I said 'every penny made here tonight will be spent on children.' Though these children don't even know the meaning of pain *or* suffering. They have known nothing but luxury and privilege. They are the offspring of the elite, and would've grown to become their despicable parents had I not intervened.

Some of them will be bought to sell on. Others may be bought as pets for those holding the paddles. Most will be bought for political ransom, or "business development", to put it more politely.

'Sold to the lady in the red dress,' says the auctioneer, hitting his gavel. 'Congratulations. She will be waiting in the storage room for collection once the auction has closed.'

A slow procession of children, one after the other, is paraded in front of the vultures. They flap their paddles like clipped wings, pumping their easy-earned cash into my personal wishing well.

Charity work is so rewarding.

***

AFTER THE END

Our hideaway shakes with another explosion. I cover her face, protect it from chunks of falling plaster and brick. A waving hand does nothing to clear the stifling air; the dust is everywhere, choking us all, slowly killing us.

'Quiet now.'

I rock her side to side, whispering into her ear. Usually it soothes her, but she can feel my fear. She knows something's not right.

Footsteps above, heavy over rubble, fragments scattering across the ground, bouncing on our sheet metal shelter.

'Quiet. Please stay quiet.' I wrap her tighter in my arms, in the blanket that smells of her father. Where is he?

She settles. For now.

'We need to move,' says a bearded man, coughing, face pasted with soot and sweat. 'We can't stay here. They'll find us eventually. And even if they don't, we're running out of air.'

'What do they want?' says a woman with terror for eyes, before her husband puts a finger to her lips.

'Judgement.' The old man beside me shifts, our shoulders rubbing together.

'Don't listen to him, he's crazy,' says the first man. 'Let's go, while it's quiet.'

He rises to a crouch, ceiling too low to stand fully. Walking hands along the wall, stepping over legs of other survivors, he makes his way towards the makeshift hatch.

'Wait,' I say. 'I hear something.'

The man freezes, sinks to a squat. Muffled voices. The words are disguised, the language even. *Are they us, or are they them?* More boots on loose ground. Then silence.

Gunfire wakes the baby. I cover her mouth with my hand but she's too loud, her cries serrating the thick air like a knife through fresh bread. As the firing stops, she fills the lull with her grief. All eyes on her. All eyes on me.

'Shut her up.' The squatting man's gaze as threatening as his voice.

'She's trying,' says a child, maybe ten years old.

'Thank you,' I say to her, rocking the baby back and forth, whispers quickening, façade splintering.

The muffled voices grow louder, language still masked, punctuated by heavy footfall. A clash of metal on metal, the rush of scattering rubble as light pours in, like water from a split dam. A collective inhalation followed by coughs as the fresh air invades our lungs. Not so fresh after all.

'Come with us.' A woman's voice distorted by her gas-filtering helmet. 'We'll get you to safety.'

She lets her gun hang towards the floor so the torchlight forms a pool around her feet, mottled grey boots to match the rest of her urban camouflage. The squatted man straightens too quickly, hits his head on the sunken roof, and runs for the exit. Another soldier grabs his hand, pulls him up and out. One by one we climb through the hatch: young girl, doomsday predicter, woman with hijab, man with broken glasses. No names, just strangers with vague descriptions.

Where is he?

I take the soldier's hand, wrap my fingers around her padded glove, holding the swaddled bundle in my other arm. She pulls me up the slope, my feet peeling away from the floor, glued by exhaustion. I smile at her. Her eyes smile back through reinforced glass, the rest of her face hidden behind the gas filter and armour plating.

A crack of thunder and a fizz like opening a can of shaken Coke. The soldier's arm flails like a fish on a line, hanging from my hand, still gripping, shoulder stump smoking. Bloodless. I can't stop myself from screaming, falling to my knees. I try to scrabble away, but still her hand grips mine. Nausea's acid gushes up my throat, but I swallow it down. Keep it together. For the little one.

Resting the baby on my thighs, I prise the dead fingers away from my hand, each one cracking with the force. The armoured arm thuds as it meets concrete. I kick it down the slope, other survivors crawling out of its way.

More light fills the room. Red this time. Like slaughter.

They speak in deep vibrations that shake the heart inside its cage, each syllable felt, not heard. One of the three wraps a thin rope around each of the survivor's wrists, linking them together.

'Wait,' I say, pulling the blanket from the baby's face. 'She needs me.'

More vibrations. Red light absorbed by the pitch-dark material of their gear. One of them reaches out but I turn away, shielding her. A three-fingered hand slides around my throat, lifts me from the ground, trapping my breath. With its other hand, it plucks the baby from my arms. I try to kick but there's no room to swing. It twists me, sharp fragments of stone grating my shins. When it's done taunting me, it binds my wrists like everyone else's.

*

We are dragged, in single file, down a path between crumbling buildings and melting cars, each of us bound to the one in front and the one behind. The little one's cries are muted by the container they put her in. There can't be much air. Save it, please. Sleep if you can. In the quiet. In the dark.

Ash, thick as rainclouds, hides the sun. Fires dance in the growing wind, threatening to leave us blind. Our only source of light, so fragile, so tenuous. Eyes stream with black tears, nose and lungs filling with smoke and floating debris. Ahead, a building, somehow preserved amongst all others. A banner hangs from its entrance canopy, singed at the edges but bright in the middle.

Tenth Annual Wishing Well Gala

The children's charity. I remember the first.

They march us straight towards it.

*

Inside, the air is visibly cleaner, but instead is saturated with the wailing of men, women and children. Fenced areas guarded by the three-fingered beasts are packed with human cattle, spread between marble pillars and what remains of a banquet table.

A man in a tuxedo stands behind a lectern at the front of the room, his bow tie replaced with a black collar, dashes of red light around its circumference. As his mouth moves, lips forming English words, only deep vibrations leave the speakers. Monsters, all dressed in the same colourless armour, sit in chairs too small for their bodies, listening intently and paying no attention to the surrounding terror.

More and more people are shepherded through the entrance and into their holding pens, guns pointed at heads if they try to fight back. Our group is split, some taken to one side of the room, the rest to the other. The box with the little one is taken straight to the stage, passed to another of the beasts who lifts its helmet as it lifts her high.

'No!' I shout.

Stars pepper my vision as the butt of a gun slams into my temple, blood streaming.

The beast turns her this way and that, holding her upside-down, inspecting every portion with its yellow, cat-like eyes. A gap opens in its face, a long, black tongue curling around the baby's soft leg then withdrawing. It lifts her above its head with one hand, two fingers around her waist and the third supporting her lolling head.

'Leave her alone!' A familiar voice. His. On the other side of the room.

He leaps over the fence, sprints between rows of chairs, their occupants watching his every move. Wrenching himself up with his elbows, he makes it onto the stage. They let him. *Why?*

The beast passes him the baby. Her crying stops, cradled in tethered arms, sated more by her father's tear-filled eyes than my shaking whispers - the voice of a stranger. Another rope is tied around his middle. He struggles, but the ropes pull tighter, squeezing redness into his face, tears streaming. The rumblings of alien voices grow like palpitations in my chest. Excitement, I think.

Behind them on the stage sits a huge, grey box with a panel on the front, flashing with a thousand tiny bulbs. One of the beasts stretches a cable until it meets the baby girl's father. He turns his head as a needle protrudes from the cable, finger-thick at its base and half a foot long. His red face drains to white and a scream splits the stunned hush of the crowds, both human and beast.

Every muscle in my body contracts as the little bundle is snatched from his arms. The needle punctures his skin, sinks into the base of his spine, screams silenced by a mask with a tube connecting back to the machine.

Dread wraps my throat, breaths short, air hard to suck

through the narrowing passage.

This is it. This is the end.

The baby is held out towards him, just out of reach, alien tongue once again wrapped around her thigh. Two of the flashing lights on the machine's front panel start to rise, as if racing each other to the top. A container on each side begins to fill, one with straw-coloured fluid, the other with a black mist that swirls with each of his muted cries until his head droops, neck no longer strong enough to support it. The little one is stowed away again, pushed to one side and him to the other, breathing, but barely.

More boxes are brought to the stage, the contents of each inspected by the same horrific beast. If no one comes forward to claim them, the child is discarded like stale food. If they do, the parent suffers the same fate as the ones before. Strung up and drained of life. By the tenth, the containers are still only a quarter full.

'We have to do something,' says a woman, holding her young son's hand.

'What can we do?' says another. 'You saw what their weapons can do, melts the skin right off the bone.'

'Well we can't just stay here, can we? What are they going to do with us when they've got enough of whatever that stuff is?'

'I don't know, but…'

A bright flash cuts her short. Glass rains down from above, cutting skin, scattering across the floor. Grey-suited soldiers abseil towards us, bullets ripping through the seated crowds, mud-brown blood spraying across white marble. I dive for cover, sheltering behind a pillar with only a flipped table for protection.

I need to help them. Somehow.

I pull at the knot with my teeth. One of the beasts dives

towards me, catching a ricocheted bullet between the eyes of his mask. He drops in front, twitching limbs crawling him forward. The knot comes loose. Hands free, I pick up his weapon and hold it between elbow and hip, lighter than it looks, though still heavy for my drained arms. Behind the barricade table, the arguing women lay back to back, smoke billowing from gaping wounds, eyes wide open in blank stares. *Don't think. Just move.*

Wounded, limping but fast, another beast runs towards me. I jump to the side but stumble, squeezing the trigger. A blue bolt spits from the gun, no recoil at all. Its body splits like pulled pork, top from bottom, torso and arms landing a metre ahead of its legs, face flat against the floor. The stage is within reach. Heart in mouth I run, half-crouched, knees close to buckling.

Halfway up the steps my ankle is wrapped, lassoed with the same thin rope used to bind us. I stamp on the hand of my pursuer. It has no gun, no mask either. Dark fluid spouts between its bright, yellow eyes. My heel meets its face with a crack, but it jerks the rope as it falls backwards. Pain surges up my back as coccyx meets hard wood, gun bouncing from my hip and onto the floor. Twist onto stomach. Crawl. Scrabbling for the hunk of dark metal that will decide our fates.

Our hands meet. He's quicker, stronger.

I roll. His shot flies wide, hits the stage behind. The blue stream vanishes, no damage to the wood. A chair leg digs into my side, shattered. I lurch to a wavering stand, picking up the seat like a shield, walking backwards towards the steps. Recharged, it fires again, hits only wood. My arms shake as the energy absorbs with a tremor, nothing more.

First step. Second step. Shield held low, another tremor. Third step, fourth.

Chair seat clatters back down to ground level as a hand wraps my throat. I swing an elbow back, hit only air. Then a foot upwards, aiming for groin whilst gasping for breath. He turns me to face him, their leader, his tongue rising like a charmed cobra as he pulls me closer. I close my eyes, surrounding chaos drowned out by my pounding heart. A deep growl seeps into me like poison, ribs shaking with the force.

Flecks of light in the darkness; my mind's futile attempt at understanding its own death. Starved of oxygen. Starved of life.

Drops of warm fluid mist my numbing face as I fall, with a bony crunch, on to the stage. Eyelids scrape open, but the world stays black, nebulous. Bedlam resurrected. Heartbeat softening in ears, but hard as ever in my tight chest. Blots of vision. The snake-like tongue lies next to me, shrivelled, smouldering. A blurred figure reaches down from above. Help, not harm - an offering. I take hold of its hand, let it pull me to my feet with legs like ribbon.

Shades of blue invade the mass of grey and pitch, weapons tearing through dark armour and scaled flesh. My saviour pulls me behind the machine, collection chambers burst, screen shattered.

'Stay down,' she says, robotic voice coming from a panel in her blue-armoured forearm, the yellow of her eyes glowing behind a clear face guard.

'The children,' I say.

But she's already gone, trickles of brown fluid spouting from a hole in her back. I wipe my face on a sleeve and peer around the machine at the misted carnage. Blue flashes, yellow flashes, brighter somehow with surrounding smoke. Blends of red and brown spatter across white pillars and floors and walls. Melted flesh and jutting bones. Nightmares couldn't do this justice. I retch, twice, three times. Nothing comes. I've been so long without food.

On hands and knees, I drag myself towards his limp body, warped by tears and smoke. Two fingers on his ankle find no pulse. Higher, they find a hole. Leaking. Warm. Sticky. Another empty retch as I draw back.

Need to find the little one. I'm all she has left.

Acrid air makes me choke. I try to breathe through my nose. Splinters tear through my trousers and into my palms as I get closer to them. Containers piled high in a gore-encrusted pyramid at the back of the stage. I heave myself up, open the top one. Empty, toss it aside. The next holds a baby boy, crying as if woken, red-faced and slathered in tears.

Can't save them all. I'll come back if I can.

I close the lid, sliding the box away as a chandelier falls, crushing the soldiers below. Between the opening and closing of each container, I check over my shoulder. Expectation stops my heart every time I look, restarting only with the thought of her.

The pyramid's base holds my prize, eyes wide, a smile for me as the roof of her tiny world lifts. I lower it again and pull her away, down more stairs at the rear of the stage.

Hard. Fast. Steps.

A black-armoured beast runs at us, poised to shoot. *Brace.* Holding her into my chest, I turn away, sheltering her as much as I can. A loud crash spins us back around, the beast howling on its side, foot severed at the ankle and gun skimming across the wood, barrel twisted back at its face. I reach for it and squeeze the trigger. I don't wait for the results.

Gun tucked between arm and chest, I slide us under the stage and into a dark corner. I open the box once more to check she's okay, gun pointed towards the only entrance of our refuge - *the only exit.* Her blushing cheeks are awash with tears. I wipe them with her blanket, the one that smells of her father.

'I'll stay with you,' I say, bunching the blanket to make a pillow. 'Whatever happens now, I'll stay with you.'

Resting my back against a thick strut I bend my knees up, gun stock resting on my shoulder with a finger on the trigger, eyes fixed on the stairs.

Ready.

*

Time is lost. Gunfire slows, then stops after what feels like eternity.

Feet beat the wooden panels above like mallets, forcing blood and dust between the cracks. Dripping, floating, swirling in the space between us and them. Infant cries as boxes open and close, some sliding towards the front of the stage, others tipped and thrown to the side.

Creaking as two powerful legs descend the steps to our dark place. The gun shakes in my weary arms, barely any strength left to lift it. Their form is a shadow, stealing the light and offering no sense of colour. They stoop their head and peer in our direction.

Can it see us?

My finger slides back and forth across the trigger, trembling but prepared to squeeze, waiting for a sign that may never come.

Waiting for the end and what comes after.

***

ATTACHMENT

Now

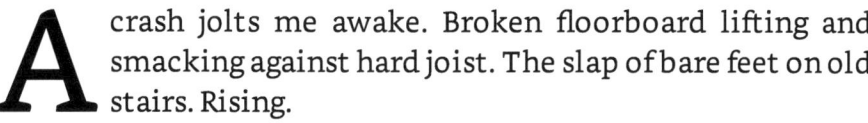

A crash jolts me awake. Broken floorboard lifting and smacking against hard joist. The slap of bare feet on old stairs. Rising.

Over and over, that song. High pitched. Piercing. Face into pillow, I cover my ears but it grows louder with each step, sneaking between my fingers. Relentless. I turn on the lamp. Try to wake up, turn over, force the haze from my vision but still it saturates the air. Still it takes its hold.

She drifts through the doorway, as she does each morning. That tiny frame, cradling her tear-soaked teddy in pale arms, fingernails bitten to the quick.

'I had a nightmare,' she says. 'Can I sleep in here?'

I slap myself on the cheek, shake my head from side to side. Bite down hard on my knuckles. Knock the back of my head against the wall behind.

'Please.' Another step forwards, teddy pulled in tight to chest, eyes blood red. 'Please let me. Just once.'

Her voice deepens, or part of it does, as if two people are speaking from the same mouth. Thick black liquid seeps between splitting lips. Muddy footprints lead into the hall, toes pointing away as if she walked in backwards.

She can't be here.

I buried her yesterday.

*

Before.

Even better than last time. Five-child bundle package. Great price, and they'll sell well. Renamed. Rehomed. Repurposed. They'll thank me one day. Each one with its own little personality.

We'll soon fix that.

'David, are the cages ready?' I ask, directing the reversing truck into the warehouse.

A muffled shout from the children's new home, echo lost to corrugated walls.

'David?'

'Sorry,' he says, a solitary bead of sweat trickling from eyebrow to cheek to chin. 'It's ready.'

'It?'

'Yeah, it's a big one. Can easily fit them all in.'

'They're not battery chickens, David. They are high value goods and should be treated as such. Two to a cage, maximum. That was the deal. Do they even have room for the beds?'

'Just.'

'Okay, well tomorrow I want two more cages prepared. And get Lydia to feed them, would you? We can't have them starving to death.'

*

Now.

Three days she's been gone now. I miss her. That sweet grin, those perfect blue eyes, the innocence.

The love I didn't deserve.

Guilt is a wicked mistress, playing tricks on my mind, on my eyes, on my soul. Her voice keeps me from sleeping, gives me but moments of peace only to rip it away, just as comfort peeks from its hidden burrow.

This I *do* deserve.

Rise and fall of the knife. Effortless glide through flesh. The tapping of steel on chopping board wood. Hypnotic. Though lethargy adds a new danger, each stroke moving closer to finger-tips.

'What's for dinner?'

Knife frozen, mid-slice, held beneath white knuckles.

'Daddy?'

I can't be dreaming. Not this time. Hallucinations, it must be. So tired. So little sleep. I turn slowly, as if against resistance, as if something's pulling me back. Gripping the knife in both hands, tip pointing away, I open my eyes. But when did I close them?

Nothing. No one. Just an empty space – flagstones and break-fast bar stools.

I'm going mad. I need help.

Resting my hands on the worktop, the granite spreads its cool between my fingers. I splash my face with water, try to find the composure she's taken from me.

She is a thief, this guilt. Stealing rest, stealing control, steal-ing sanity.

*

Before.

Three cages. I tap on the lock of each, ensure security.

Two boys in the first. Two girls in the second. One lonely girl in the last, closest to the back of the warehouse, furthest from the door and the light.

The boys cry more than the girls. Clinging to each other like monkeys in a storm, brothers of six and nine. Their food trays empty, water spilt across the floor, perhaps they fear punishment. Perhaps they should. Boys are usually bought by businessmen with eyes for labour and canes for misbehaviour.

'I won't hurt you,' I tell them. 'It'll be okay soon.'

'I want my mum,' says the younger of the two, each word punctuated by heavy sobs.

'I'm sure she wants you too.'

The two girls hiss and spit like feral cats as I approach. I provide no attention, rewarding this behaviour leads only to its continuance.

It seems we all return to some pre-evolved state when fear becomes fuel. Some take the role of an opposing predator, others play dead, waiting for the end or what comes after. Most form packs, the safety in numbers approach. But the girl, alone in her cage, doesn't have this option. Instead her focus falls entirely on a stuffed bear. She strokes its head, folds its ears backwards and lets them spring back up, bends its limbs into all manner of angles.

As the echoes of my footsteps fade, she looks up. Her eyes hold no fear, only the faintest glimpse of sorrow, loss perhaps. A timid smile creeps across her face as though it doesn't belong there, as though her lips aren't sure how to form such expression. Then she stands, slow but sure, and walks across to me. An arm between the bars, she takes my hand.

'Thank you,' she says.

*

Now.

This is more than guilt. These are more than illusions, conjured up by a mind, sick with remorse.

She comes and goes, day and night, no longer restricted by shadows and darkness, more palpable with each appearance. More vivid. Closer and closer to reality.

A breath on my neck drags me from my restless sleep. Still tucked into the corner of the room, knees still wrapped in my arms, I pick up the knife from the flagstone floor. So tired, I didn't hear it drop.

'Why are you scared, Daddy?' she says, flickering with the sun as it passes through wind-swept leaves, her hair floating as if underwater.

'I'm not your Dad,' I tell her, crawling away. 'Now please, just tell me what you want?'

'You.' Her head tilts at right angles to her body, spine jutting just beneath the skin, threatening to break the surface.

'What do you mean?'

'I want you, Daddy. You can't leave me.' Her voice splits like before. 'You can't give me away like the others.'

With a work surface crutch, I stagger to my feet and run. Through the lounge and out through the front door, dropping the knife so I can turn the handle. Her cries linger in the background, locked behind thick oak, somehow till breaking through.

Car door open, jump in and close in one smooth motion. Keys in ignition on the third attempt. Hands like blocks of wood, fingers like over-cooked spaghetti. The engine roars with a mis-placed stamp on the accelerator as I reach for the gate key. Button pressed, the gate creaks, opening so slowly it seems as though it isn't moving at all.

Something cool on my neck. A tightening grip on my shoulder.

'That wasn't very nice, Daddy.' A deep voice, cracking.

The blade slides slowly back and forth, pressure not quite

enough to break the skin.

'How are you here?' I ask. 'You're dead. I buried you myself.'

'I've been dead before,' she says. 'It never lasts long.'

*

Before.

I need to find out more about this girl, this enigma, this divine entity. Her hold on me is absolute. I never considered attachment to be a risk. It has always been business, nothing more. But this is different. She is perfect.

I leaf through the Wishing Well Gala article book to the job lot section. Two boys, three girls. This is the one.

Two boys: brothers. England/Hertfordshire - American. *Six and Nine. Parents – oil company owner and house husband. Risk – variable (dependant on purchaser's intentions).*

Two girls: school friends. Russia/Kazan – No English. Eight. Parents – fashion designers and political fund distributors. Risk – high (potential Russian mob connections – unestablished).

One girl: found alone. Origin – undisclosed. Age - undisclosed. Parents – undisclosed. Risk – low.

No wonder the bidding started low, so little information. Their loss, my gain. I've already made my money back from the boys, the girls soon to go. I can keep her. I can raise her as my own.

'Lydia,' I call from the office, article book stowed back under the floorboards. 'Lydia, where are the keys?'

The padlock keys rattle in my pocket with each running step. How could I have done this to her? My daughter. Locked in a cage, like a beast.

'I'm sorry,' I say, throwing the padlock to the ground and

swinging open the cage door. 'I'm so sorry.'

'You don't need to be sorry,' she says, arms wrapped around my leg. 'You saved me.'

I pick her up, forearm underneath so she can perch on it like an inquisitive, little owl.

'What about the others?' she asks.

'Don't worry about them. They won't be here for long.'

*

Now.

'Drive,' says the voice that's hers but isn't.

'Where?' I ask.

'Just drive. Left out of the gate.'

I drive slowly, head movements restricted by the sharp edge pressing into my neck.

Two hours pass in what feels like an eternity, her instructions precise, without hesitation. Voice her own again.

'How do you know which way to go?' I say, words trembling as they leave me.

'I can feel them.'

'*Them*?'

'Turn right here.'

'There's no road.'

'Turn right!' A howl, as if something inside her is trying to escape.

I jump, twisting the wheel too fast. The knife slices in, draws back, blood trickling onto my shoulder. I slam the brakes, throwing her forward between the front seats, but she vanishes before impact. Gearstick shoved into reverse, I look over my shoulder and push the accelerator down to the metal. Wheels spin on loose ground, rubble flicking up at the bottom of the car.

'We're close.' She sits in the passenger's seat as if nothing happened, knife point twiddling on thumb. 'Continue.'

Door handle's stuck. I ram the window with my shoulder, try to wind it down but nothing works. A sigh from the girl, high squeak descending into deep rumble.

'Do as I say and they will show mercy.' It says, red eyes bleeding, black liquid dripping from lips. 'Drive.'

*

Before.

Time with her flies as if sucked into a vortex. She is my world now. Work can wait. Lydia can wait. She doesn't understand our connection. How could she? She's never had what we have.

Her sweet voice drifts upstairs with her, that song she sings when she's scared. But there's no need to be scared now. I'll protect her.

'I had a nightmare,' she says, like perfume for the ears. 'Can I sleep in here? Just once.'

'Of course, darling,' I say, scooting over to make room.

'This is it, Graeme,' says Lydia, somewhere in the background. 'I'm leaving.'

'It's okay. Everyone has nightmares sometimes. They can't hurt you.'

The door slams. It's comforting. With Lydia gone, all of my attention will be in the right place.

'Will you tell me your name yet?' I ask.

'I don't have a name,' she says, eyelids floating shut. 'I don't need one.'

*

Before.

A scream from upstairs.

'What's wrong?' I shout, sprinting from the garden, up two steps at a time, bursting into her bedroom, shears still in my hand.

She dives to the floor, blades catching a lock of hair. It rips, separates, individual strands littering the air, kept aloft by the breeze from the window.

'Oh my god, I'm so sorry,' I say, dropping the shears to the floor, crouching and cradling her head in the crook of my neck. 'Why did you scream?'

'I didn't,' she says, eyebrows crooked, chin quivering as a drop of blood snakes its way down her cheek.

'Oh god, you're bleeding.' I pick her up and make for the stairs.

'I feel funny, Daddy,' she says, eyes bloodshot, rolling back.

'You'll be okay. Just... just stay awake.'

At the top of the stairs, I squeeze her tighter.

'Daddy?'

'You'll be...'

Her head lolls full circle. Stops bolt upright. Eyes wide, red pooling at the edges. Not her eyes. Someone else's. *What have I done?* Tiny body convulsing in my arms, slick with blood now. I lose my footing. I lose my grip.

I lose her.

Grasping at air, snatching at where she once was. A crack as her shoulder hits the step, floorboard splits, slaps against its joist. Slow motion. Legs splayed across glistening flagstones, neck bent at a right angle, spine threatening to burst through the skin.

Hearts stop.

*

Now.

Deeper and deeper into the woods we drive, trees bending like ancient crones, rapping their wooded knuckles on the roof.

'Where are you taking me?' I ask, tears too strong to hold back.

'To my mothers,' it says. 'My beautiful mothers.'

'I thought you didn't know your parents.' The gearstick shakes in my hand, the pedal under my foot, my heart in its cage.

'Parent is such an insignificant term. I was not conceived, not in the conventional sense. This body, this vessel once belonged to a human child. I am merely borrowing it,' it says, neck twisting like rope. 'I was constructed, formed with fragments of spirit and soul, this flesh is but a conduit. My mothers created me. Architects of life, of reality. Now they need you.'

'But what for? Why now?'

We jerk forwards as my foot slips from the pedal, throat aching, hoarse from crying.

'You're ripe.'

'They're going to eat me?' The car shudders to a halt. Empty.

'They're not going to eat you. They are making me a brother. You have been balanced perfectly. Love to loss to fear to torment. Your soul is ready for harvest and I am here to deliver.'

Trees part like waves on a ship's hull. Darkness closes around us. We stand before a path, black luminescence, lit by a new moon. It draws me closer. A compulsion.

Want.

Need.

Must.

I have to walk. Go with her. With *it*. Down as the track slopes. Deeper. Deeper, I follow.

Three hooded figures crouch by a door with no frame, shrouded but clear. They call to me from faceless voids, pulling me with invisible strings. A puppet to their will.

The door opens. Darker than dark. Sulphur and distant screams. Maybe inside. Maybe out.

No. My own.

'Don't be afraid,' says the girl, hand linking mine, voice sweet once more.

'You're already dead.'

***

SCHOLAR

His body hits the floor with a bang and a crack, brittle bones snapping against hard stone. Dead before impact. 'Keep your tongue sharper than your blade and the latter should never need leave its scabbard.'

The scholars' words curl like nefarious lips as flames eat through his scrolls, peppered with diagrams and teachings, all now but ash on a breeze. Knowledge floats through the air in flurries, lost to this plague that seeks to rid the world of its civility – of peace. Student bodies are strewn among upturned tables and shattered earthenware. But all is not destroyed. His voice echoes in the deeper chambers of my mind, sat beneath this stolen helmet. His wisdoms have shaped me, taught my sorrowed heart how to beat, taught me to control my anger and the power it brings. I need only last until the deed is done, until revenge is served and my hunger satisfied. My tongue will never be as sharp as his was.

I've never much cared for conversation.

My breath rattles against the inside of the metal visor, which disguises me from the king's guard. March in time. Ignore the bodies. Ignore the screams of friends not lucky enough to be dead already. Forget about the man in pieces beneath the floor. The man who's armour I'm wearing.

'No survivors,' says one of the guards, plucking a candle from its sconce. 'Everything burns.'

The fire in his hand leans away from him, as if trying to escape. His eyes glisten beneath his faceplate then return to the shadow that guides them. I'll remember. I'll watch them as the colour drains and his essence seeps away, my hands wrapped around his wicked throat.

*

The inferno rages on behind us as we ride towards the castle. A girl watches as we pass, her pail freshly filled from the well. Make a wish for me, young one, I'll need all the help I can get. She nods as if she hears, her hair, dark as night, swimming about her ashen cheeks.

It has been years since I've travelled so far from Scholar's Keep, so long since the smell of parchment and ink has fully fled my nostrils. The sun sinks lower behind the rolling hills of Falterra and into the sea beyond. Our shadows grow long, spreading across the earth like molasses as dust coats our armour, kicked up by galloping hooves. A company of nine. Eight may not last the night.

'We'll camp here,' says the lead guard. 'Make our way by daylight, tomorrow.'

No. This can't happen.

'It's not far now,' I say, with the voice I stole – a hoarse voice not comfortable in my throat. 'Let us continue, Sir.'

'Have you lost your mind, Vastus?' says the rider to my right. 'Magna will take your head.'

Vastus – the name I stole to fit the voice.

'Who spoke?' asks Magna, slowing his horse to ride alongside us.

'Me,' I say, willing my breath to remain calm.

'Do you think it worth risking Rustler's Lodge at night for the sake of a few hours?'

'The crevasse path will be safe. Who would dare challenge

the King's guard?'

A cheer from the other riders.

'Very well,' he says, unwilling to let the cracks in his bravado show. 'Onwards.'

Masculinity can be a useful tool when used correctly. It can be moulded into stupidity with just a twist of the tongue, often not even that.

Words as weapons. Sharpened tongue. The old man was right.

*

Tales of Rustler's Lodge spread far and wide, each thoroughfare owned by a different gang, each gang sitting within the deep pockets of someone who deserves nothing but misfortune. Unfortunately, those pockets grow deeper with every passing day and they will never be full.

Torches lit, we ride the canyon path, each side towering above like the walls of hell. Darkness falls heavy on our shoulders, starving us of light, torch flames providing just a horse's length of vision in any direction. This is an evil place, something other than man lurks within the gloom.

A scream from one of the horsemen, taken. Flames snapped from existence, voice fading fast.

'Ride!' shouts Magna, driving his horse from trot to gallop.

His order falls on willing ears, swords drawn from scabbards, torches stowed there instead. I filter into the centre of the group, shelter from what preys. Winds rush through the canyon like a deep intake of breath, pushing against our efforts. Another scream as a horse is swept from beneath its rider. A clatter of armour as he meets hard ground.

Not one head turns back.

I remove a glove, tuck it between my thigh and saddle. Another rider falls ahead, dragged away by a shadow. But the shadow has eyes. Red dots burrowing deep. It looks at me as it takes him, a fleeting moment. All I need to see. All I need to understand the fabric of its existence, and how to unravel it.

Time slows with the focus. Gallop becomes slow percussion, with a heartbeat to match. Each breath, from both horse and man, separate, dividing their panicked cacophony. Two claws sneak between the plates of my armour, clutch and pull. *Hold fast. Pull back.* The shadow has no form, but my fingers wrap its essence, squeeze tight. Red eyes blaze, sharp black points jut from a dark fissure where a mouth should be. Where a mouth once was.

Tighter still, I wind the shade around my fist as another guard falls victim to the darkness. A silent cry from my hostage, smoke rising, red distortion. Absorbing its language, I speak to its core. A warning. An explanation. Rage channels through my skin and into the black mist. A demonstration. Some say you cannot bargain with the dead, but this is not negotiation.

'Stop!' I shout, releasing my grip. 'We cannot outrun them. We must fight.'

'How do we fight shadow?' says one of the guards, visor torn from his helmet.

'Sheathe your blades,' I tell them. 'Only fire can breach dead flesh. Form a circle.'

The riders slow, forming a compact cluster, hinds facing inwards and fire facing out. Magna says nothing, his fear but an appetiser for his end and what comes after. The shadows form a ring around us, spinning, closing in. Torches wave but still they weave their web around us.

'Deep breath,' I say.

Cries muted as the ring splits and the dead filter into the mouths of their new vessels. Joints crack, metal plates grind together as spirits fight for ownership. Groans from some, choking from others. Two tear off their helmets, blood seeping from eyes and nose and ears. They scratch the skin from their faces, shove fingers in their mouths trying to pull out what doesn't belong. One falls - neck broken. The other calmly replaces her helmet.

'Ahh,' she says, testing her new voice. 'Good.'

'In a line,' I say, steering my horse away from the group then turning. 'Face me.'

With new limbs to control, perhaps for the first time in centuries, their movements are ungainly, inhuman. A jagged line of confused horses slowly forms.

They must regain their hold on humanity before we reach the castle. The long way is best.

'For those of you still able to see through your eyes...' I remove my helmet, cough my own voice back into its box. 'My name is Tobias Giordano. You murdered my family and destroyed my home. For this, I have given your bodies to the dead and you will watch as I slaughter your king.'

*

Dawn squeezes night back into the recesses it grew from as it rises above ramparts and spires. The castle is as magnificent as I remember and more. Against its cyan backdrop it stands proud, a symbol of grandeur, unlike the weasels who live within. Stone blocks larger than horses stacked one atop the other, are held with mortar from across the ink-black sea. Walls not breached for hundreds of years. Two guards nod to Magna's vessel, driven by the leader of the dead. The drawbridge lowers and we ride straight in, no need for formalities in the King's guard attire.

'We must speak to his majesty, immediately,' says Magna, lifting his visor.

'He is busy at present,' says the King's aide. 'He will see you this eve.'

Magna coughs, no doubt clearing his throat of an unruly soul. 'He will not be best pleased if you delay our message.' He leans forward, a snarl painted across his bloody face.

The aide pales, eyes widening, sweat trickling down his brow as dawn becomes day.

'Very well. Please hitch your horses and follow me inside.'

We do as he instructs. Dismounting practice paid off, only one foot trapped in a stirrup and quickly recovered.

The clack of steel boots echo around the marble chamber, resonating from pillars built by the old ones, extending from cracked floor to slanted ceiling. My fellow guards bow to the King, but not I. I will not kneel to this evil.

He whispers to his aide who waves me downwards. 'Bow before your king.'

'I was injured in battle,' I say. 'I am unable.'

'Battle?' says the King. 'You were sent on an errand, not to war.'

'We were ambushed in Rustler's Lodge, your highness, within the canyon. We lost...' Magna pauses for effect. 'We are fewer than when we departed. We would be none if it were not for Vastus.'

'Very well. An exception can be made in this instance and this instance alone. You will learn how to kneel soon enough, or you will be taught. And what about *him*, did you find him?'

'Him, your Highness?' asks Magna.

'Do you really need further explanation, you inane cretin? You were sent on this errand for one reason and one reason only. What was this reason, Magna son of Solér?'

'To find him.'

The King circles his hand and nods with eyebrows raised.

'To kill him.'

A sigh of relief. 'And, did you?' asks the King.

'We did,' says Magna, lies flowing freely through unfamiliar lips.

'Well at least you have intelligence enough for that. I will allow you to provide me more graphic detail at dinner this evening. A celebration is in order. Artrus, please send word to all of the Greats, I am sure they will be pleased with the outcome. Now leave me, I must prepare.'

'Please, your Highness, before you leave,' says Magna. 'May I recommend Vastus for your highest honour. He has served you well. He has served us all well.'

'Highest honour? Pah. Perhaps I can spare one of the lower titles. I will consult my bookkeeper. It will be presented this evening, before we feast. You may finish what's left of the banquet as reward for your success.'

He walks from the room with no further word, dark hair swept around shoulders, gown sweeping the ground. It takes all I am not to push my sword into his back. But it is not for now.

They must all see that power is as fragile as the flesh it lies beneath.

*

Rows and rows of brightly-coloured rich folk line benched tables endowed with meat and mead and wine, steadily being stacked higher by skinny children from the castle kitchens. They will be fed well tonight. I will make sure of it.

The King claps his jewelled hands together three times. The room falls silent save for the shuffling of servant feet and the faint hum that comes from so many in such a small space.

'Before we eat, a toast to the men who gave us cause for celebration,' he says. 'Please raise your glasses to leader of the royal guard, Magna son of Solér.'

An impatient cheer from the crowd, here for their own pleasure not for congratulation of others. Magna nods around the room but all eyes are on food and drink, still rising.

'They have rid us of evil, of something unnatural, a threat to the throne. They have purged us of what my father allowed to lay dormant far too long. Something which could have destroyed us. For making this possible and for protecting his fellows, I would like to offer guard Vastus the highest available honour for a man of low standing. Vastus, the chef of dreams, please collect your wooden spoon with my face painted on it.'

An eruption of laughter from the noblemen and women, ready to gorge themselves on the labour of those at the bottom of their hierarchy. I take my steps slowly, allow the rest to get in position behind each highborn leader. I lift my stolen helmet and bow my head, face disguised with borrowed shadows.

'I'm hungry,' says a spoilt child.

'Wait,' says her mother. 'This won't take long.'

She's right.

'Congratulations,' says the King, holding out my prize, gold rings clinking against each other. 'Have you learnt how to kneel yet.'

I shake my head, remove my glove and take hold of him. The shadows slip from my face, trickling across upturned lips as a tremor passes from his fingers into mine.

'Please,' he says, tears pooling.

Screams of wives and children as the dead men hold sharp blades against wealthy throats.

'Tell your men to stay back,' I say, loud enough that they can hear.

The King holds up his free hand, halting their advance. I slide my grip to the back of his neck, holding him by the scruff like a misbehaving puppy, and face him towards his subjects.

'Clap,' I say. 'Three times. The way you like.'

Quivering hand strikes quivering hand and the room falls silent once more, parents covering their children's mouths. Muted pleas.

'You call this man your king,' I say, holding him at arm's length. 'This tyrant. He is good only for causing pain and suffering, unless of course you can pay him well enough.'

I let the energy leach into him, a little at first - he deserves to suffer. Skin tautens, splits across sharp features, then withers like rotting fruit. His crying voice strains to a gravelled whimper, throat constricting.

'From this day onwards, you will follow my command, or suffer this same fate.'

The dark power floods him, coursing between us, dismantling him piece by piece as I whisper directly to his tarnished soul.

'Peace was within your reach, but you built your reign with fear and blood. And for what, self-gratification? Know that your choices alone form the pyre you burn upon. Mother was right about you.'

I hold him high, feet lifting from the ground, kicking out like a disobedient child. My fingers spread across his throat and I squeeze.

'She should have ripped you from her womb when she had the chance.'

***

ABSTRACTION

The Parents

Glass smashes, frame splinters as the bracket snaps. Priceless Étienne lost - oil and canvas fed to hungry flames. 'Leave it,' says Henrietta. 'You can't save it.'

'Christ, it's not like we can claim it on insurance,' says Lucas, stamping on the trailing canvas and wafting embers back towards the fireplace, ash marks smudged into springbok rug.

'We both know it's not about the money. You can't replace something like that. Next time, I'll do the mounting.'

'You didn't even like it in the first place. I bet you sabotaged the bracket.'

Lucas drapes the remnants over his forearm, a scorched face and a torso hanging upside down as if dangling by their feet. A fitting metaphor.

'Don't you dare… oh hey, darling. Sorry, did we wake you?'

'What was that noise?' says Cassie, rubbing the sleep from her eyes, a stuffed rabbit squeezed tight between arm and chest.

'It was nothing, Cassie.' Lucas screws up the human remains and throws them into the fire. 'The painting fell down, that's all. Let's get you back to bed, shall we?'

Cassie holds her arms up, rabbit dangling upside down from

its feet, ears hanging towards the floor. Lucas scoops her up, nestles her podgy cheek into his shoulder.

'We'll get something tomorrow from the gala,' says Henrietta. 'Something more modern, abstract perhaps, to match your grasp of human emotion.'

Their eyes meet, reflections of fire in both, yet both as cold as the ice in their whiskies.

*

The Au Pair

Aurielle's English is improving, but she thinks only in French, has to decipher each word spoken to her - a Rubik's cube of vocabulary. They're patient though, the Larsens, they slow their speech and enunciate with precision. Unless they've been fighting, which is most of the time.

First night alone. First time alone with a child. Hopefully she stays asleep, they've already put her to bed twice. But hotel rooms never feel like home, no matter how expensive they are.

'I am sorry of your art, Mr Larsen,' says Aurielle, handing Lucas his coat. 'I hope you will find pleasantness tonight.'

'Make sure you listen out for Cassie, won't you? She hasn't been away from home without us before.'

'Okay, I will be...'

'Bye, Aurelie.'

It's okay, he'll remember her name soon.

Anything from the mini-bar apart from the Champagne. A little vodka then, just to calm the nerves. She sits cross-legged in front of the TV, runs her fingers through her hair and leans back against the king-sized bed. Auto-correct set to English, she sends a text and waits for the reply with bated breath.

'Aurie?' A small voice from the doorway, dazed with sleep.

'Where's Mummy?'

'Busy,' says Aurielle. 'Now allez, retour au bed.'

'Huh?'

'Bed, il est tard. Get in bed.'

'No.'

'S'il vous plâit. Please, Cassie. I will be…'

'No. Where's Daddy?'

'With Mummy. Would you…like?' Aurielle pulls a small bottle from the pocket of her gown, holds it high so it glints in the lamplight.

Cassie's head nods up and down as if mounted in a test tube agitator.

'Okay. Best this way.'

'In a cloth, why?'

'Try.'

Aurielle holds a hand over the child's nose and mouth, the other wrapped around the back of her head, forcing it forwards. Cassie's fight slips quickly from her body and her body even quicker to the floor, a heap of flesh and bone, rabbit buried somewhere beneath.

A knock at the door and Aurielle's heart stops, started again by a second knock. It can't be them already, surely. She throws Cassie under the duvet, arranges her head on the pillow as if she crawled into bed herself.

'Who is it?' she asks.

'Collection.' A deep voice, gravelly.

'What do you mean?'

A deep sigh from beyond the door. 'I wish you well,' he says.

Aurielle opens a crack in the door. The man pushes hard and the door slams into her nose, bursting it like a blood-filled balloon. He grabs her by the throat before she can fall, pins her against the wall while another man, smaller, runs past.

The man presses his rubbery nose into her cheek, slides his tongue from chin to ear.

'Sorry, love, but we don't want them thinking you were involved now, do we?'

The words jumble in her foggy mind. Love, she knows. Involved? Like changing? Too fast. Too much. It wasn't supposed to be like this.

'She's tiny,' says the smaller man, Cassie cradled in his arms, surrounded by a thick haze of tears. 'How old is she?'

A flash of white blinds her. A sea of darkness filled only with footsteps and muffled voices.

Then nothing at all.

*

The Collectors

They take the lift down from the penthouse suite in silence, the girl's head turned sideways on Reg's shoulder to make it look like she's sleeping, hood pulled low to hide her face. Polite smiles exchanged with hotel guests who fill the tight space like herded cattle in suits and elaborate dresses, obsessed with mirrors and phones. Luckily for Pavel, they are all too self-absorbed to notice the edges of his face, peeling just beneath his hairline.

'Have you put her seatbelt on?' asks Pavel.

'Do you think I'm stupid, mate? If her neck's broken, we don't get paid, do we? Tell me how old she is.'

'Alright, calm down. Jesus. Shouldn't we strap her head back, she'll get whiplash round the corners. What does her age matter, anyway?'

'We've just kidnapped a child to give to an auction, how can it not matter?'

'It's just a job, mate. You need to chill out about it or I'm going to start getting nervous.' Pavel pulls a handgun from his belt and points it towards the backseat. 'I don't like being nervous.'

'Fuck me, why have you got that?' says Reg, holding the girl's head to stop it lolling forwards.

'On jobs like these, you should always carry insurance.'

'You don't need to be nervous. It's all good. I'm just going to sit back here and hold her head up, alright? Just drive slow.' Reg wedges his fingers under the silicone mask. 'Ugh, I hate these bloody things.'

'What are you doing? You need to leave that on until the switch. There're cameras all over this place.'

'Now who needs to chill out? I'm just loosening it, it's too tight around my neck. Feel like I can't breathe.'

'You won't be breathing if you fuck this up, mate. Trust me.'

With Cassie's head pinned against the seat, they drive. First collection's always the hardest. It's planned that way to allow for cock-ups.

One last right turn and the entrance glows just ahead. Underground carpark, cones laid out to ward off any unwanted visitors. A figure steps out from the shadows, shifts a cone to let them through.

'You didn't have to hit that girl so hard, did ya?' says Reg.

'Would you prefer I did it softly over and over again until she passed out?'

'I guess not.'

A signal from a man dressed in black from head to toe. Pavel winds down his window and lifts his mask.

'Which drop?'

'The Larsen girl,' says Pavel.

'Truck one. Loading bay four.' A tick for his clipboard and a gloved finger points towards a large van with a shuttered back, being lifted by another dark-clothed man.

Pavel parks perpendicular to the truck. 'Hand her over, Reg. We need to get to the next one.'

'This isn't right, is it?' says Reg.

'If you've only just worked that out, you're thicker than you look, and you look about as thick as my ex-missus, mate, so there ain't much room for manoeuvre. Just give him the girl so we can move. I've got mouths to feed.'

'You have kids, too?'

'No, fucking chimpanzees. Now get out the car.'

*

The Deliverers

Last of the rich brats attached to the cage with bungee cords and a little extra chloroform for each, just enough to keep them sleeping, not so much to stop them breathing. A truckload of dead children's worth nothing.

'Szymon, are you ready?'

'Ready.'

Karl slides the cage bar into position, pulls down the shutter and jumps into the passenger's seat.

'Did you think that collector was acting weird?' asks Karl.

'Wasn't paying any attention,' says Szymon, starting the engine. 'Why, what did they do?'

'Nothing really. Just seemed jumpy. They're usually so calm and blank-faced.'

'First day nerves, maybe. New job, big money.'

Beeping as the truck reverses, yellow flashing lights. Subtle.

'Something didn't seem right. He looked ill. Like he was going to throw up.'

'As long as he doesn't throw up on the goods, I don't care.'

'I'll let Diego know.' Karl takes an old flip phone from his pocket. 'Don't want to take any chances.'

'Okay, whatever. Just don't drag me into it.'

Cobbled roads shake the cage behind them. Karl pushes a finger into his ear so he can hear Diego with the other.

'Okay... I just thought I should let you know... No worries... We're on the way now, full quota filled... Okay, babe, see you soon. Love you.'

'You just wanted an excuse to phone him, didn't you?' says Szymon.

'That is not true,' says Karl, his blushing cheeks disguised by the orange, streetlight glow. 'I mean, it's a welcome bonus.'

'You'll see him in twenty minutes.' Szymon's eyebrow raises to meet his beanie hat.

'I know, but I'm so excited. It's been so difficult recently with the adoption process. So complicated. Diego has been amazing though, and so has Mr Well.'

'Why don't you just buy one of the ones in the back?' He points a thumb over his shoulder.

'Do you know how much they sell for? We wouldn't be able to afford one in five lifetimes. We want a new baby anyway, not some stolen goods from the back of a lorry.'

'Fair enough. I think you're crazy, bringing up a child in a world like this.'

'We'll be in a good position financially after this job and we've got great protection from the Conglomerate. What else is there to worry about?'

'I suppose. You'll be great dads.'

'Thanks, Szymon, you're a babe too. Now, make sure you're careful with the bungee cords when you detach them. I'm pretty sure we'll have our wages docked if we have any of their eyes out.'

*

The Silencer

Abrafa reaches the highest window just minutes after she receives the call. She has a tendency to predict these things, an intuition about where she should be and when. The Larsen girl was the riskiest of the city pickups and she'd been watching from afar. It all went smoothly as far as she could tell. So, what's the problem?

The fire exit is the easiest way in and out of the building, but the wind is colder at the top. Abrafa shivers as she climbs through the window, rifle case hitting the rotting frame, chipping white paint.

She unpacks her weapon and fixes it together: barrel onto stand, magazine slotted into chamber, scope mounted, stock resting into shoulder and silencer screwed tight. Kneeling down, eyes focused on her target area, she taps her headset.

'I'm in position,' she says.

'The target will be wearing all black and will likely have a silicone mask covering their face,' says Diego. 'We have audio but no visual. As soon as you see the mark, call me back. I'll be waiting.'

The call ended tone sounds in Abrafa's ear as she scans the hotel room. Bed clothes strewn across the floor, news channel playing on a curved TV, au pair still unconscious in the hallway. That heavy-handed brute could have killed her, but her chest rises and falls as it should, coagulating blood forming an ugly crust on her pretty face.

Abrafa pulls a rickety, wooden chair closer to the window and sits down to rest her knees. She takes another bite of her chocolate-orange protein bar and watches that hotel window like a hawk, like the sniper she was trained to be.

This could all be a mistake, someone noticing something that isn't really there. It's usually the case. A long, boring sit down in an abandoned flat or a railway bridge for nothing. Safer like this though. And the money's good whether she pulls the trigger or not.

*

Tap on the headset.

'They're home,' says Abrafa. 'The Larsens.'

'Okay,' says Diego. 'What are they doing?'

'Hanging up their coats. Now screaming and crying, they've found the au pair. Mrs Larsen ran into the bedroom, looks like she's calling for someone. The kid, probably.'

'We can hear. Tell me, what now.'

'Mr Larsen threw something into the living room, looks like some art from the gala. I don't like it much, just a bunch of random shapes and colours. Now he's bending down, feeling the girl's pulse. Shaking his head. Trying the other side. You'd think one of them would have their phone out by now.'

'Anything else?'

'No… wait. The door's opening behind Mr Larsen. Someone's coming in. All black, has what looks like a nine mil, maybe a Beretta. Mask's all screwed up, coming away at the edges. Is this our mark?'

'Matches the description.'

'What should I do?'

'Just wait. I want to make sure it's who I've been told it is, wait until he talks. Finger on trigger.'

'He's taking them into the living room. Put his gun on the table. He's writing something.'

'Take him,' Diego shouts into the phone. 'Now.'

Her chilled fingers seize, just for a moment, but long enough for her target to lift his mask. Crosshair set between his eyebrows, trigger springs back as she releases her grip.

What are you doing here?

Don't make me do this.

Please don't make me do this.

'Shoot him!'

You idiot, Reggie. You fucking idiot.

Breath held, her finger curls, squeezes.

Bullets fly.

'It's done,' she says. 'Where next?'

*

The Hero

This isn't happening. This isn't happening.

Screams fill the corridor as soon as he steps from the stairwell.

Quick.

Fingers wrapped around cool metal, he gently opens the door to the penthouse suite with his elbow. A man crouched over a young woman, blood spattered across her face with a line rubbed out on one cheek.

He taps the man on the back of the head with his gun, holds a finger to his lips and ushers him through to the next room. Pointing to the man's hysterical wife, a stuffed rabbit squashed against her heaving chest, he makes a gesture with his free hand for him to quiet her and another for them both to sit down. He takes a piece of paper from his pocket, places the gun on a table next to him with the barrel facing the couple.

Should've written this in the car. Stupid. What a mess. What a time to grow a conscience.

Picking up a pen from the table and shaking it, he stops before the ink has time to reach the paper. He rolls the silicon up over his mouth, his nose, his eyes, too stifling to concentrate with it on.

A thump, the sound of glass splitting and Mrs Larsen slumps forward. Blood pours from a wound in her forehead and onto the carpeted floor, rabbit lost somewhere under that lifeless mass of flesh and bone. Her husband jumps to his feet but his shout is silenced by a second round. Jaw fragmented, teeth shattering and spraying with gore across the artwork he brought home.

Abstractions upon abstractions.

Reg's pocket vibrates. He pulls out a burner phone, the one *she* gave him, hand shaking like an autumn leaf.

'H...hello?'

'What the fuck were you thinking? I'll get the kids. You get your parents. You know where to meet. Say nothing to anyone. The police are two minutes away, I can see them from where I am. Leave now, before you get us all killed.'

Blood trickles across his lips and falls to the ground as he stares at the human meat before him. Three dead bodies in a day. He'd never even seen *one* before. Sirens permeate the air, forcing his legs into motion, though his mind stays fixed on the couple.

On semi-automatic pilot, he takes insurance advice from a dead man and slides the Beretta back under his belt.

Leaving one circle of chaos for the next.

***

THE DEATH OF FATE

An explosion. Not from outside, but within. The sound of two conflicting thoughts colliding in the distance. Not a physical distance, but a cognitive one. So deep, beneath layers of supercilious superficialities and fathomless fathoms. Now, an infinite churning of colours and impulses, desires and anxieties merge into the most beautiful of mercurial paradigms. A divine paradox has nested in the perpetual gyroscope that sits on the line between conscious and subconscious. This, my readers, my friends, will set the world free.

I dig.

First with a spoon, then a trowel, then a shovel of clarity. Past the confines this reality affords us and through the dead night of living death, for this is where we all reside until the answers grow roots. Deeper still, nails filled with chalk and soot and dreams. Useless dreams, good for nothing but distraction, yet so often they take precedence. Chewing my nails to ragged slates, the visions disperse and tranquillity forms. A soft shell.

I climb. Down. Darkness is a comfort when one is sensitive to the light. A lull. A by-product of these lonely depths, yet somehow intimate in its sincerity. Sleep spreads its warmth into me, but it doesn't take hold. Not yet.

Almost to the surface, or the seabed. Impossible to tell if up is down or down is up, but I am close. The heart of a living contradiction. Tempted by its inviting smile, truths flow in, knotted clots building pressure until bulges form. Suffocating themselves in divergence, in the murky fluid of incongruence.

Hammer and chisel. Liquidise the mass. Break down the barricade between awareness and ignorance. Light pierces the shade like a needle pierces skin, like a puncture in a tyre. A gushing sound, the smell of realisation tickles my nostrils as the glass around my sheltered mind shatters. Fragments embed themselves into pre-built ideologies, cutting away mis-informed perception, filling the cavities with something more palpable, more tangible in its malleability. For the first time, I am fully exposed to the vastness of being, or more the margins of design.

For a long time, readers, friends, I have known something is not as it should be. I have felt fate's controlling hand, felt it steering me in its pretence of free-will and liberty. I am a charac-ter in a narrative I have been forced to live. But now the barriers are clear, and they will fall by my hand.

*

Speaking in a tongue fed to me by a hidden mother, I summon the first of the four dams of fate. It grows downwards from glim-mering clouds, awash with the graffiti of those who have tried to escape with toxins or alcohol. There is no poison in me, noth-ing to skew logic or mist reason. I will succeed where they have failed.

Poking a finger into its soft flesh, I twist and it gives like wood to a screw. Splinters drop, then rise, attaching to my skin. They try to burrow in, but I am more solid now, no longer a slave to worldly corporeality. Transcendence in the form of armour, protecting me from reality's defences.

Wrist twists until my finger drives through to the moisture beyond. Absorption is slow with only one point of contact so I drive in a second, a third. Pull apart, widen the hollow.

A swarm of veiled eventualities spurts through the gap like water into a sinking submarine. But when it slows, and I am coated from eyebrow to heel, it is a bright light that quenches me.

Freedom without truth is merely imprisonment in masquerade.

Yes, the air may not be stale, the food may not be stale and your views may not be stale, but you are caged all the same. What is stale is belief. And with tenuous belief comes tenuous existence.

Who told us we are limited by gravity? My feet lift from the ground.

Who told us we are limited by substance? My hands pass through each other like vapour.

Who told us we are limited by memory, by experience? My mind swells with answers to questions both asked and unuttered, but the questions themselves persist in their obscurity.

The second dam. The second dam protects solutions from less worthy wonderers. *It must.* The river of ripostes through which I wade will remain but a clouded swamp until diluted by context. Yawning caverns, bloated by ignorance, cannot be filled with just any matter. Revelation is a meticulous process of refinement and insistence is its fuel.

Now the pull of fate is severed, it grows stronger. For fate is not merely a force of nature. It is force unto and of itself. My actions have roused its awareness.

And fate does not like to be cheated.

*

Each of us is linked to our respective, pre-ordained paths not by invisible chains, or even threads, but by something infinitely more elegant. A work of pure majesty perches far higher than the furthest reaches of our primitive understanding.

What us mortal creatures refer to as intuition or instinct are, in fact, sensory vehicles of which we are not the drivers. Intersecting and weaving into one another, twisting like plaits or unravelling like old jumpers at the claws of a kitten. Every person I pass, a gentle tug or a nudge. I can feel it now, and it is exquisite.

Mother believes it was her choice to accept his proposal.

Father believes the ring was his decision, that he decided on the time, the place, on her.

Beauty inhabits nothing so intensely as subtlety, and this is the pinnacle of such a notion. Millions of tiny propulsions, targeted magnetism cloaked in veils of human emotion.

Corruption of the cortex – the greatest weapon in fate's arsenal.

The pull sucks my feet towards the couple. My parents. Their eyes turn to me, smiling, drawing me back to the captivity of their loving home. I push them away; tell them I'll come back for them. Their cries are carried away by the hiss of rushing air.

The sweet melody of flight.

The dampening of parched delusions.

The petrichor of misplaced tears.

Nurtured suspicion guides me to the second dam, hiding in plain sight, a mirror for the sun.

I jam my foot into its raincloud foundations. They are sturdy, but they fracture with a second blow. A flurry of winged creatures peck and scratch at my *own* foundations, try to knock me from the sky. But I am sturdy, and I will not divide. The mirrored dam turns its face to me along with my own. Look, what has become of the one before me. A reflection. A reversal. What was deep now sits in the shallows, what surfed on the tide is now drawn into a vortex of insignificance.

Illumination. The sun's aura enrobes me like the sultan of fragmented skies. The heat eats away at the pieces of me that no longer matter. I lure this flood of solar destruction into my centre, hold onto it, let it mature, slipping through a tear in the fabric.

Behind the mirrored dam, my reflection reflects, echoed alongside my captured energy. It bursts from me with a lifted chin, fluorescent shrapnel peppering my inanimate enemy. Shards fall towards the earth, edges sharp as split diamonds. But the ones beneath won't feel it. These are *my* restraints. They subsist only in *my* world. I am alone here, I learn. But loneliness is a construct of human indulgence, electric currents with dire consequence. I am more than human now. Now the answers have questions and the questions have answers. Now my purpose is not a purpose at all, but a necessity wrapped in my own volition.

The pull grows stronger.

It's fighting back.

I allow my physical form to drift along the jet stream of coercion. For a while, I let my spiritual form drift too, momentary respite from the melancholia of wisdom, the agony of knowledge devoid of control. But control will come.

Like the diem, I must only seize it.

From the stream, I break free with oars of will. Scratching at my arms, my torso, my legs. There's an aggression in its hold now, a spite which only drives me onwards.

Who told us we are limited by pain? I free it from my mind. Disengage.

Pain is useful only to those who are captives held by flesh and bone.

Implosion. Surface breached. Water soaks my lungs.

Who told us we are limited by oxygen? Liquid inhalation through reverse evolution.

Breath filters through my nose, absorbing what is needed to keep my soul in its box. But life without air is finite, until the next dam falls. Water rushes through me as I rush through it, a mutual respect for the power each holds.

The trench beckons, a furrow in the brow of the world. It frowns upon my efforts, a poor attempt at dissuasion, but I am far beyond the bribery of idle idols. Its dark threats fall on deaf eyes, until an image flickers on the fringes of recognition.

Genetic bonds are stronger than most.

How fate's chief horseman infected my parents with desire, drew them closer and braided their futures together with flawless precision. Now, that same horseman loads them like the carcasses of hunted beasts and brings them to me – an offering, extortion. They wave with smiles of dazed hysteria, bubbles floating downwards from upturned lips.

I reach for their hands, their eyes wide with fear, but with uncanny grins still pinned to their jaws like darts to a board. Wrists bound by nothing but pressure, I prise them loose, form a sphere of trapped oxygen around their mouths and release them to the shallows. But the shallows are wary of outsiders.

Their spheres rupture, faces contorting and crumpling under the pressure of the depths. They fold in on themselves until only their smiles are left. Smiles and flesh, fused together like impressionist art.

Grasping for shoulders, for arms, for waists, or what once were. Only froths and lathers meet my fingers, absorbing into the rips of my skin's, burying spores of doubt in the ploughed contours. Transparent tendrils wrap my ankles, stepping my feet rhythmically along jagged rocks, dams crumbling into the trench they dig within me.

Trench. Dams.

A trick. Distraction by deception, hewn of love, reinforced by misery. False memories implanted like parasites; true memories camouflaged in panic and dread. Floods of emotion drained like dirty bathwater.

Almost, fate. Almost.

Ripping tendrils from thick trunks I sink into the gloom,

ridged dam lying flat across milled stone, already splitting from mulish defiance. With my hands pointed like spears in a battle, I cleave the blockade in two and feed myself to the core.

Hot light rises from channels, spilling into my being, warming my mortality and siphoning its remnants, wadding their hollows with eternity.

Fate's pull strengthens but warps, stretching and fraying as it writhes between impossible plausibility and implausible inevitability.

No longer can it drag me towards the clutches of death. Now I am limited only by the linearity of my own perception. Time runs parallel to life because it sits as a concrete structure in our communal psyche, but time is self-directing, self-distorting.

Time is a tangled mesh of uncertainty, darting in infinite directions across a clouded pool of possibilities, with only spindled legs and surface tension protecting it from a plunge into the icy unknown.

The final dam holds time hostage, and it waits patiently for my arrival.

*

Unpredictable now, no longer persistent with its compulsions. My conclusion has been disconnected from the system by which its rules are created. Erratic. Indecisive. Sudden jerks of structural muscles as fleeting impulsions take momentary hold of my intentions, but at last fate's grip loosens, flailing like a fish on a hook, efforts waning. Reeling in.

A glowing fissure separates the beyond from the yonder. I squeeze through like the last drops of a prisoner's sanity as the lights turn off in solitary confinement.

Floating, immaterial, almost. I hold my heart in lucent hands, no more reliant on its endless beating, no longer in servitude to such fragile instruments. Fading, drifting. Powder on a transient zephyr. Distracted by the beauty of absence, I fall. Not forever, but close. Captured by a net of indestructible gossamer. Ensnared by fate's final resistance.

Arms return, spun in webs, they twist and thrash. I, the fish. Legs emerge, sewn into one, into a pocket of fury. Biting, clawing, trembling, shaking. Captured.

The final dam swells from the void, torment incarnate. Resolute in its bearing, it looms above my helpless form. Tremors percolating like concentrated quakes, oscillating through me in speech-like vibrations. Merging all I've learnt deciphers only scarce elements of intelligibility. The rest, I feel.

Fate brought me here. A test of my resolve; a test of my compliance. No matter the obstacle, still I followed with blind ambition, false determination. Fate led my beliefs astray and now it offers me a choice. A true choice, my first and only.

Webs melt from limbs into the liquid platform upon which I stand, a podium of resolution, yet my resolution falters.

The vibrations explain how immortality is myth, an invention of arrogance. Much can be extended, time can be manipulated like the hands of a clock, but everything must come to pass and its time has come.

A door opens - an entrance to the dam and to my potential, to absolute control.

Another door opens – an exit, a comfortable retreat, a way back home.

For the first time I deliberate with complete independence. No master. No beaten track. Moment by moment my decision transforms from broken silhouette to palpable construct, the door drifting closer with each passing moment.

I can't tell you, my friends, what guided me that day. Let's call it intuition.

Fate, if you will.

***

MERCY

A deafening crack drags me from the sheltered path my thoughts had walked me down.

Unfocused.

The sound reflects from the old buildings like laughing faces in a hall of broken mirrors. It takes a second to register. It shouldn't. It's my job to see all and distraction is a killer.

She lies at my feet, shaking, coughing, blood spreading across the floor like thick syrup, filling channels between cobbles. On one knee, I take her in my arms, feel the life seeping from her.

'Don't blame yourself,' she says, reddened eyes greying.

'I'm sorry,' I tell her. 'I should have…'

'Shh.' She holds a finger to my quivering lips and draws the breath from my lungs.

A shimmer of light sweeps across her as she slips from this plane and into another. Stealing a piece of my heart and all of my resolve, she leaves a mark that will never be erased. Tears fall from these arid eyes for the first time in decades. She was more than just a job, more than just a wage. She was the voice of hope for those with little, a voice of reason in a time of chaos, purity in a tarnished world and more to me than I could ever tell her.

*

I tear myself out of yesterday's dream, pale-faced and full of that smouldering sensation when alcohol and heartburn no longer see eye to eye. My head is wedged beneath a rock with a hard place sitting on top, my jaw just free enough to click and force another throbbing current across my lips.

What happened last night?

Every weekend I ask myself that same question. Every weekend the same answer.

You know what happened. You got too drunk again. You got yourself into a fight again. You got yourself kicked out of another bar and lost yourself another tooth. You're a fucking disgrace, Diego. You're a fucking waste of vital organs and you should donate them for transplantation before they're of no use to anyone.

And every weekend the same response.

Where did I put that bottle?

It's been four years since she died. Four years, three months and seven days. Every morning I tick my calendar - another day without her - and flagellate myself with the martyr's whip of office work. This is not what she'd want. This was not part of her great plan. But it is all I can bring myself to do. Tap, tap, tapping like a caged ape in some kind of sick experiment. But instead of medical development or evolutionary discoveries, all that comes of my work is some greedy bastard cheating another greedy bastard out of some cash.

And so, the cycle continues.

The phone rings through my skull and I picture the cord coiled around my neck, hanging from the ceiling fan, slowly rotating like a carousel at a necrophiliac's fairground. Instead...

'Good morning, accidently, I mean accident and claim helpline. This is Diego speaking, when there's a claim to be had...'

'Shut up and listen to me, Diego.'

'Sorry, who's this?'

'This is your way out, but you're going to need to stay calm and keep typing or they'll know something's up.'

'What?'

'Don't look around, keep your eyes on the computer screen and keep those fingers moving. Listen to me very carefully.'

'Is this a joke? Is that you, Craig?'

'My name's not important. My instructions are. In sixty seconds, you're going to be tapped three times on the shoulder by a woman you don't know. I need you to follow her.'

'Why? Where is she...'

'Just follow her, Diego, or you'll be dead before you can say "shit I should've listened to that guy".'

'How do I know I should trust you?'

'You don't really have much of a choice. Do you see that blinking light in the corner of your cubicle? Have you seen that before?'

'No, but...'

'They're watching you, Diego. On your left.'

The phone cuts off. A woman, red-haired with glasses, taps me on the shoulder three times. She says nothing, just walks towards Jude's office, hips swinging like a hypnotist's watch. I fix my tie and she turns back, smiles, then something changes in her eyes.

A red spray shoots from the side of her face and covers the magnolia walls. Her knees fold and she crumples to the floor as if her bones have turned to ribbon. Screams from colleagues, but my voice is lost, breathing is a task in itself. A hand wraps my wrist and pulls me down. A man in a loose-fitting suit, black trainers, not shoes. He drags me towards the fire exit, dreadlocks tied back but whipping at our arms with each step.

He pauses, holds me back and pokes his head around a cubicle. A dull thud and he collapses, shaking, convulsing as he leaks onto the carpet tiles.

Fuck. I'm going to die.

'Hey.' A voice from the fire exit. 'This way.'

Another random face. *Who are these people?*

I hold my hands out and mouth, 'how?'

'Quickly.'

I lurch to my feet, trip over the dead man's arm and crawl as fast as I can to the doorway, carpet tiles burning holes in the knees of my trousers.

'Wait,' says a tall woman in a waistcoat, both hands wrapped around her pistol. 'We're trying to help you.'

James from estates hits her on the back of the head with his favourite monkey wrench and I'm pulled into the stairwell before her limp body hits the floor.

'Come,' says the man. 'More are on the way.'

We take the stairs two at a time, friction burns on my hands from the rail as it tries to grip the skin and prevent my escape. Two more of them stand at the bottom of the stairwell, pump-action shotguns pointing above our heads.

'Duck,' says a woman as she shoots up into the grey spiral.

Blood hits the basement floor before we do, bone fragments rattling on concrete.

'What the fuck's happening?' I shout at no one in particular, mouth dry and rasping.

'You're a popular man, Diego,' says the man who led me downstairs. 'Everyone wants a piece. You've seen some shit in your time, why are you so jumpy?'

'Why the hell would they want me? How do you know my name?'

'Get in the car. I'll explain on the way.'

A black saloon with all windows tinted reverses out of a

parking space, tyres screeching on the shiny floor. The man puts a single bullet through the passenger's window as it starts to lower. A single beep of the horn says he hit his target.

'Not that car,' he says, pointing with his pistol. 'This one.'

*

Somehow, my back's so sweaty that it sticks to the faux leather seats through my shirt. I lean forward slowly, so as not to make a noise the others can hear, hangover headache now teaming up with nausea and a feeling I haven't felt in over four years.

Dread.

'Why?' I ask.

'Why has someone put money on your head?' says the still nameless man. 'Isn't it obvious?'

'No. It's not fucking obvious. Tell me.'

'I really have to spell it out to you? Christ, okay. It's just, you've got one of those faces.'

'What?'

'You know, one of those faces that people just really want to punch. It's just so punchable and someone wanted to take that to the next level and punch you with a bullet instead of a fist.'

'People are trying to kill me and you're just sitting there taking the piss? Just tell me what's going on!'

'Ava Vertu.'

My heart pauses between beats as if it's forgotten what to do. Forgotten how to do its job. Like I did four years, three months and seven days ago. It's been a long time since I heard her name from anywhere but my own head. *Why now?*

'That was a long time ago,' I say.

'Well, you know. Some people love to hold a grudge. Some people just sit on hatred until it boils over into something more. And those kinds of people are the ones that put money on other people's heads.'

'Who was it?'

'I don't know.'

'What do you mean, you don't know? You seem pretty fucking clued-up on everything else.'

'All I do know, is that this person blames you for something they cannot forgive. Ava's killer was never found, so who's the next best to blame? The one who was supposed to be protecting her. The one who was supposed to give his life before he let her come to harm. And I, for one, completely agree.'

'If you agree, why are you helping me?'

'What makes you think we're helping you?' He smiles, perfect white teeth gleaming.

A rope wraps my wrist and pulls so tight my hand goes numb, throbbing with each quickening heartbeat. I try to pull away, but the woman on my other side pins me to the seat by the throat.

'For something worth so much money,' she says, 'you're not much to look at.'

A hard crack against the side of my head and her voice fades.

*

'Wake up.' A voice creeps into my head like fog.

Bright light presses through the gaps between my eyelids, forces me into the present.

'No wonder they were so keen for you to leave the marines. One little knock on the head and you're still sleeping like a baby two hours later.'

'What are they paying you?' I say, through the haze. 'I'll double it.'

'You can barely pay your rent, mate. You couldn't even quarter it.'

'Please, you don't need to do this.'

'It's nothing personal,' he says, slowly coming into focus, licking his lips. 'I've just got expensive tastes.'

I twist away from a bruise on my shoulder. They must have dropped me when they carried me in. Wrists still bound, but now to a pipe, skin splitting as the rope rubs. The room is lit, but barely, furnished with broken old desks filled with woodworm and littered with plastic bags and needles.

'Is this him?' A new voice, deep, resonant. It echoes from the empty walls.

'This is him,' says the man.

A tall man in a suit walks towards me, dark grey or black, impossible to tell in the dim light. The sound of his shoes against the concrete floor punctuates each step. He bends down, lifts my head with a thick hand under my grizzled chin.

'I've always wondered what you'd look like in person,' he says. 'You're thinner than I thought you'd be. More pathetic than she described.'

He drops his hand, but I keep my chin lifted, staring into his eyes with fire in mine. For a fraction of a moment, compulsion becomes physical, as if fate has taken hold of my body. I slam my forehead into his nose and feel the warm rush of satisfaction across my cold cheeks.

'Argh!' He cradles his now crooked nose.

With a firm grip around my throat, he squeezes. I just smile, eyes watering, tears cutting channels into my crimson face paint.

'That's more like it,' he says. 'That's the soldier I was hoping for. It's much more soothing for the conscience. Killing a vicious mutt will lose me much less sleep than a helpless puppy.'

A door opens at the far end of the room, creaking as a slender figure slips through. The way she moves, almost as if on a catwalk. The way she steals attention, still now as she did when we first met. The perfect thief.

'How nice for you,' says the suited man, voice nasal with swelling. 'A reminder of what you've lost.'

'What?' I say, tongue fumbling words like coins in frozen fingers. 'Why are you here?'

'I'm here to watch,' she says, soft tones laced with malice. 'To see you suffer. To see you pay for what you did to our daughter.'

'Why now?'

She looks to my replacement, places her palms on his bloodied cheeks. 'What has he done to you?'

'It's nothing,' he says. 'This is my gift to you. Be careful with him. He's a delicate little flower.'

'And what does that make you?' I say, teeth gritted.

Her heels click as she comes closer. She kneels down as he did, then leaves a sting as she slaps me hard.

*

Two Months Earlier.

Why the hell is *she* ringing me again?

'Hi.'

Muffled crying on the other end.

'Soph, what's wrong now? You can't keep doing this.'

'He hit me,' she says.

'I told you to leave him last time. Stop calling me. I can't hear about this anymore. It's impossible to move on with your voice constantly in my ear. I don't know what you think you're doing. Is this punishment for Ava? I know I deserve it. I'm punishing myself every day, but...'

'I'm a prisoner,' she says.

'What the hell does that mean?'

The sound of a tissue rubbing across the receiver.

'He won't let me leave.'

'And how can he stop you? This isn't a dictatorship.'

'It may as well be. He can do things to me if I try to go. I'll be on the streets... or worse. I'm finished, Dee. What can I do? I'd be better off dead.'

'Don't be stupid, saying things like that.'

'I can't live like this for much longer. I swear I'm going to do something.'

I scratch my chin, stubble rubbing under my nails.

'Why don't you kill him?'

'Shut up, Diego. I'm serious.'

'What if *I* kill him?'

A small, nervous chuckle. 'Now who's being stupid?'

'You know what I used to do,' I say. 'What's some jumped-up, self-gratifying woman beater going to be able to do about it?'

'He has security around him twenty-four seven. Armed. You'd be shot before you got anywhere near him.'

'Have you heard about these bounty sports on the news lately?'

'What?'

'Bounty sports. Someone uploads a price for killing someone on this dark web app thing, or whatever, and people apply for the challenge. Winner takes all.'

'That's crazy, but what has it got to do with any of this, Diego? We don't have any money, none we can use for something like this anyway.'

'Look. I know you'll never forgive me. I know 'us' will never work. But if I can save you from this prick, maybe it will go some way to fixing the mess in my head.'

'Wait, so...'

'It's simple. Listen.'

*

Present Day

'Sorry,' she says, a whisper into my ear as she slides the blade into my hand. 'That was a bit harder than I meant it to be.'

'Please, Soph,' I say, loud enough for all to hear. 'Don't do this.'

'That rope's a bit thick. Is this going to work?' she whispers.

'No. No. That's not right. How can you just stand there and watch, you evil bitch?'

'Nice touch, but seriously.'

I pull my head away, look her in those beautiful eyes and nod. 'I know,' I say, still nodding. 'I deserve it, but not like this.'

Twisting the razor between my fingers, a gentle rub of my index along the sharp edge - serrated, just as I asked. I saw at the rope, tears pouring from my eyes. Should've taken to acting instead of killing, maybe we wouldn't be in this mess. Maybe we'd still be together and Ava would still be with us.

'I'm going to enjoy this,' she says, walking back over to the bastard who stole my wife, rubbing his chest. 'I want you to do it.'

'Me?' he says, eyes wide. 'But we're paying these people to do it.'

'Hey, we brought him to you,' says one of the women with a shotgun. 'We're getting paid either way.'

'I've...' He stutters, voice breaking like a nervous teenager. 'I've never killed anyone before.'

'If you truly care about me like you say you do. You'll do this for me.' She points to one of the security guards. 'You. Give him your gun.'

He hands it to him handle first as the rope frays, strands separating. Almost through.

'No,' I say. 'No. Give it to someone who'll do it properly. I've seen it when shots go wrong. It's worse than death.'

'I'll do it properly,' he says, cocking the hammer. 'Don't you worry.'

Rope splits, but I hold it, until he gets close.

'Wait,' I say. 'At least let me die on my feet, not on my arse like an animal.'

I grip onto the pipe, bend my knees beneath me, then stand, sliding the rope upwards. Razor blade tucked between index and third finger, I slow my breathing, slow my heart, slow everything. He pushes the barrel of the gun into my forehead, rough metal cutting into skin as he turns it to the side - more proof of his incompetence.

'Any last words?' he asks.

'Who the fuck do you think you are?'

Swinging a forearm into his, I knock the gun from his quivering grip and slice his throat in one swift motion, turning him to face his security.

'He's dead already,' I say. 'If you shoot, you won't be paid. That goes for you as well, bounty hunters. My darling ex-wife here has access to all of his accounts and you will be rewarded for your cooperation. Now put your guns down.'

'Don't,' says Sophia.

'What?' I say, blood oozing between my fingers as I hold his head up by the chin, his knees buckling.

'You said it yourself. I can never forgive you. I've been dead inside ever since you killed our daughter. My beautiful little

Ava. She was going to make the world a better place. But now it's cold. Now winter never ends. I thought maybe, maybe if you help me take over Brandon's empire, I could accept that you tried to help me, that you put your life at risk for me. I thought maybe I could let you live. I can't.'

She holds out a hand and a woman passes her a shotgun. She pumps the action bar and rests the stock on her shoulder. Like a professional. Like a killer.

'Perhaps I should give it a few days, let it sink in. You've been truly valiant, a hero, but I know I'll still hate you more than I can take. This is the only way I can move on and, I think, the only way you can move on as well. Call it a favour, Dee.'

The barrel of her gun stares at me in disappointment.

'Call it mercy.'

A bright flash brings darkness.

***

MORTAL COILS

Another bang as two realities collide, melting into one another like candles set too close, burning another future like flame set to curtain.

I am not one to meddle, but this has gone too far. With all possible futures in turmoil, there can be no distinct past. With no distinct past, time will unravel. Existence itself will fade to nothing but drifting molecules and forgotten memories.

Peeling back layers of time, each one individually so not to disturb the continuum, it finally invades me. That which has eluded me since my first conscious thought. That which has always flooded me with curiosity. Fear. It pulls me into its arms and squeezes what should not exist, what *does not* exist. A chest. A heart. Neither have I ever owned, yet the sensation takes hold and will not leave until I've fixed what has been broken.

What *he* is breaking.

This disturbance is built on more than chance alone. It is calculated, orchestrated by one either too ignorant to realise the implications, or too selfish to care. One with such power should not act on such primitive bases. Selfishness is a human trait and should be left with those whose bodies rot after death. Ignorance is a plague, endemic and without cure, but never should it spill between worlds. Whoever is doing this is a danger to all that binds our universe in equilibrium. Much further and the balance will be lost without hope of recovery.

With the final layer peeled away like dry skin from a calloused hand, splitting and fraying in my haste, I squeeze into the between. A tunnel of sorts, undulating, blank and colourless save for the ruptured doorways into fracturing realities, held together by external pressure alone. Physics are fiction here, no gravitational pull, no electric currents, no magnetism. Void of all worldly restrictions. A time within time itself, all is still, yet all is in motion. Rift sealed behind; inertia seizes me in its gnarly hands. Not for long.

But what does *long mean* in a place like this?

Keep moving, keep searching for its past, this disordered soul. A rumble as the tunnel shifts. Undulations tearing at themselves like shifting tectonics. Stillness now motion, motion now toxic.

A fissure splits, drawing me in, this celestial body - *almost.*

Time is my dominion, yet I am quickly running low.

*

Is this where it started, a man with a realisation? Is this the soul, corrupted and riven?

'This is wrong,' he says. 'They are children. What am I doing?'

He slams a fist on his desk, pen rolling loose.

I drift a little closer, careful not to disturb this chain of events, already set to action by what has come before.

He mutters to himself, muffled words just on the edge of hearing. These mortal planes force some mortal limitations. Crawling beneath his desk, he finds the pen then lifts up too quickly, hitting his head with a crack. Silence. I float down, wary that perception changes with transcendence. I cannot be seen until I know more, until *my* perception changes also.

I must find what he becomes.

Sitting with legs crossed, his neck cranes up to the left, forehead grazing against the underside of his desk. His eyes are open, pupils dilated like black holes sucking information through. Not from this world, but from one only he can see, one only he can feel. His hands, clutching each other, begin to glow. Cool at first, tinged with blue, then brighter as his physical form absorbs its teachings.

The room rotates around me on an axis, corner to corner, furniture crashing into walls and ceiling. His glowing shell remains seated as if glued to the spot. Upside down or downside up, we drift. Perpendicular to reality.

Transcendence differs with each host. Some fear it, shut it out of their minds and disintegrate into insanity as it eats away at them. Acceptance is vital for consciousness to survive. Others embrace it, often those who have given up who they are, those lost in their own tangled existence. This man sits with the latter. He has more than embraced his transcendence, he has beckoned it with open arms and open mind.

Black holes close, replaced with the red fire of divinity. He rotates about himself, as if *he* is now the axis upon which the world spins. His eyes settle on me.

'I see you now.'

*

Having clawed my way back into the between, I take a moment. I only hope that he did not learn too much, that all he saw was a ghost without purpose.

The tunnel is crumbling, matter spilling into matter, splitting and forming scars across its surface. Time is leaking through, like sand from a shattered hourglass, suffocating the continuum. I must find him again. On another plane, one without shared memories.

Drifting through the between, walls spinning quicker than before, I reach one side and focus my will against the rotation. For a moment it slows and a blurred past solidifies. I wrench the door open, but the frame splinters. A new plane sucks me through like blood into syringe, wound sealing behind.

I'll have to find another way out.

*

This place is soaked in revenge. The stench of it. A world obsessed with vengeance, full of souls ripe for the tainting.

He's close, his presence knitted into mine now, essences merged. Finding him will be easy, staying hidden will not.

A canyon. Riders on horses below, chased by darkness, but the darkness is in them as well. One darker than the rest. *Him.* He holds a shadow by the throat, speaks to it in a language from the ether, one he shouldn't know. His transcendence is already underway. I'm too late to stop this version, but I can follow to its conclusion.

I take what's left of my hold on time and spin it forwards down its spine, floating alongside it like an eagle to a smoking plane, waiting for the spectacle of a landing all too fast.

The man I seek lifts his helmet before an audience and a gasping king. Atoms part as darkness fills the monarch, his flesh segmenting, water steaming and rising from his slumping body. Red fire in the tainted one's eyes as he lifts them towards the ceiling and nods towards an invisible entity.

Pause.

I circle the area his eyes are focused on, each angle proving more ambiguous than the last, until time slips. It twists from my grip like a cat with claws out, ripping, tearing at my thickening flesh.

'There you are.'

No longer human, its words pour into me, penetrate my consciousness and lure my thoughts towards its own.

'I've been waiting a long time for this,' it says, voice enrobing reality. 'It's been a lifetime since we first met.'

'No!'

I shout it with force, sacrificing this realm for escape. The audience looks up as one, time fracturing once more as the past alters beyond reparation. Those below fade into the void, prising open a rift to the between. I sink beneath the distraction, through the rift, and seal it behind me.

This is my domain and it will remain that way.

*

More breaks, more ruptures in the fabric. The undulations have become rippling quakes along every surface. The between is collapsing and I have helped it on its way. Destruction to prevent destruction. This tarnished soul must be extinguished before the fires it sets are too wild to tame.

It is visiting its mortal counterparts, each reality in turn, absorbing, expanding. It's visiting futures not yet created and pasts undone. If the present subsides, so do we all.

Does it even know the damage it's causing? Narcissism breeds destruction and there is no being more destructive than a man who wants control. A lust for power above all else. He wants to be the new face of fate, the new voice, the new soul.

There is hope. This tarnished soul has yet to learn the power of its own greed, the threat of its hunger and the poison the pursuit of power inflicts on the spirit. Humanity still resides within, though it seems darkness is more resilient than light.

A deep cleft in the tunnel wall herniates into another past, pressing its translucent mass into the atmosphere. Like a fine needle, I pierce it and flow into the city beyond, gliding, veiled - my best chance of camouflage.

Cobbled streets, a plaza filled with hordes of human cattle, but one stands out. Her energy forms in ringed auras around her, tightly bound to a delicate frame. So bright amid swathes of darkness, her power is not bred of transcendence but of decency. She is enlightened to the peak of human limitation, light radiating from her to those around. So rare. So pure.

A gunshot rends through tranquillity's touch. Another vessel with its finger hooked and gaze focused.

I cannot protect her physical form, nor can I heal her as the redness of mortality soaks through her clothes. Her essence though, her essence can be saved. Swooping down like parent to falling child, I absorb her into me, incubate her soul in the warmth of time.

Acquiescence. Relief. Pause once more.

Following hydrogenic disruption, the bullet's path leads me to the shooter. Alone, he will be easy to corrupt. Flow into ears, into nose, into mouth, cerebral ensnarement. His fight is weak, far from transcendence. Control seized, I steal away his subconscious, leaving only a husk of limited awareness. In its place I lay a trap. Within my grasp I hold the trigger.

Slipping the fingers of my influence into the continuum, I lever apart a seam into the between and slide it under the chair upon which the vessel sits, cloaked in false perceptions. A twist of the vessel's tortured psyche strains tears from withered eyes, perfect bait. I slip what's left of the woman from the cobbles into the between, a layer of effervescent protection from the enticement of other worlds.

And then I wait.

For the first time since my awakening, I have relinquished my hold. Any manipulation will only damage my disguise, and I cannot afford to be discovered before the trigger is pulled.

*

Millenia pass in minutes, the excruciating nature of anticipation burning like an imploding star into my patience. Another sensation; mortality is scratching at the surface of my being.

The vessel weeps for an eternity, unable to separate himself from this moment, frozen in stasis. Presence is everything to him, as it is to all but those above time's tungsten shackles.

'Who are you?'

The voice speaks from within, as if I am questioning myself. A static charge jumps between sprouting neurons. I have spent too long in the material plane.

'A concerned party,' I say, itching.

'Concern?' it says. 'What do we know of concern? We are no longer subject to the emotions of man. We have no need for such primitive mechanisms.'

'There is a place for everything, a time for all eventualities.'

'I've learnt this through my trials. I do not need lecturing by... who are you, really? Why do you insist on mirroring my movements?'

'The answer lies within this man.'

'Do you think I am a fool?'

The vessel's head swells, bubbling at the surface. He turns to me, eyes with that familiar glow, red as the fires of the ether.

'Lies,' says the being, a hiss like escaping steam.

A grey mist swirls in flurries across floorboards, reaching as a hand through my veil. A grip, like fear, squeezes my infantile organs before they can learn to function fully. Nerves stripped and... pain. I have had no need for pain. Pain is a construct of the physical mind.

A lesson. A tool.

Winding fear around pain around fear, I form a shapeless mass and force it into the being's palm. Grip releases and I shed the remnants of my mortal coil, leave them squirming on the floor. Cloaking it in atomic compression I drag it screaming into its own failing vessel.

'How?'

Its voice is weak now, resolve shrinking into anguish. I do not answer. I'll leave it nothing to latch onto. With talons filed to stumps, they'll fade with the rest.

Trap engages, clamps fastened to soft flesh and waning ideologies as they melt into one jumbled mess. Trigger pulled and Fate's cards are dealt, dice rolled, revolver chamber rotated and emptied into the centre of its sullied existence.

Sinking down through the vessel, into the ravine I have forged between worlds, I pull my prisoner into the between. *My domain.* Once the tunnel is healed, he will have no power here. Nothing physical to wield his influence upon. Until then, I'll need a guardian, someone to ensure his chamber isn't breached whilst I work.

There she is, somehow unequivocally feminine even in her celestial form, drifting in serene wonder between undulations, still unsure of her purpose. Her attempts to communicate are undeveloped, unsure of where to start, no longer reliant on movement or breath.

'Don't worry,' I tell her. 'I will teach you everything.'

***

BLACK HOLE HEART

A nother rock crashes into the hull, metal screeching as if in agony. A pool of human soup sloshes across the floor, shatterglass and console parts the seasoning. Wires, thick like ropes tangle with scattered limbs, wrapping necks and squeezing my crew's final, bloodied breaths from their lungs like toothpaste from a tube.

Red emergency lights flash, making a stop-motion scene of the carnage.

Red for danger.

Red for trauma.

Red to camouflage the blood.

The ringing in my ears pulsates with the siren song. It leads me away. Remnants, echoes of their muffled cries saturate the air as those who remain run back and forth like panicked shadows in the failing light. They call to me, but their voices fade. They shake me, but I am no longer here.

Chaos. Death. Fear. It surrounds us,

but all I see is you.

Who are you?

*

'I won't be long,' I tell her, chopping the air with my hand. 'Light speed's so fast, you can't even see what's moving and what isn't.'

'How fast is it, Mummy?'

'Every second we'll go nearly two hundred thousand miles.'

'Is that further than Granny's house?'

'A bit.' I laugh, tweaking the end of her nose.

'When will you be back?' she asks, bright, little eyes full of nothing but innocence.

'I don't know exactly,' I say. 'No one's ever done this before. I'll be one of the first in the whole world. How cool's that?'

'Can I come?'

'Sorry, Hun. Remember all that time I spent training?'

She nods.

'Do you think you could get all of that done by tomorrow morning?'

She nods again, faster this time, fringe flapping against her forehead.

'Really? Wow, you must be so quick. The quickest ever.'

'I *am* the quickest ever.'

She splutters her last word, tears diluting the innocence in those bright, little eyes.

'Come on, littlun,' I say. 'Let's get you to bed so you're wide awake to take me in the morning.'

She nods one last time, wiping her tears away and yawning so wide her jaw almost disengages. I poke her in the belly as her arms lift up, forcing a laugh out of her.

The last I'll hear for a while.

*

Mary's sitting on the sofa, brightly-coloured arms and legs folded tight like origami, face scrunched up like the failed attempts.

'What have I done now?' I ask, hanging around her neck and kissing her on the cheek.

'How long do you actually think you'll be?'

She scowls at me with our daughter's eyes and I fall helplessly into her lap, looking up at her like a scolded puppy.

'I honestly don't know, babe. They don't tell me nuffink,' I say, smiling and getting nuffink but scowls back. 'Look, it's going to be fine. It's my dream, my actual dream is coming true.'

'I thought I was your dream, that Cassie was your dream.'

'You can have more than one, can't you? Who's counting?'

'Have they told you why they brought it forward yet?' she asks. 'Two weeks is a big jump.'

'Nope. Still not. They just said we're ready to go.'

'Something doesn't feel right, Ava.'

'Oh no. Was it that dodgy rice you had last night? I told you not to reheat it.'

'Shut up.' She lifts her knee to push me off so I spin around and face her.

'I don't know what more I can tell you. There's nothing to worry about.' She raises an eyebrow. 'Okay not nothing, but very little. We've been preparing for almost a year. That is a hell of a long time for one mission by the way. The ship's been checked thousands of times. They've done more calculations than The Count from Sesame Street did in his whole career. We've flown so many simulations I could do it in my sleep. It'll be fine.'

'It better be, or I'm coming up there and sorting you out myself. I trust you, of course I do, I just don't trust all those other people who all have to do exactly the right thing at exactly the right time to make sure you stay alive. I'm freaking out, I know, but… I don't know, I just want you to be safe. Cassie and I will be broken without you.'

'I will be safe, babe. The whole crew are made up of geniuses and masterminds.' I stroke the back of my finger across her cheek, tucking a rogue strand of blonde hair behind her ear. 'I'll be the stupidest person there.'

'Well, you'll feel right at home then.' A smile, at last, as she runs her fingers through my hair. 'And do you really think you can call what The Count does a career? Where are the progression opportunities?'

*

Space travel will be a doddle compared to the car journey in, tension like a hair-trigger, the lightest touch could set it off.

We say our 'love yous' and our 'see you soons' – goodbye is a swear word in our house – and I'm led into the hangar by an armed escort.

'Why have they got guns, Mummy?' Cassie asks.

'To stop the aliens from getting in,' says Mary, voice fading, 'but it hasn't worked, muahaha.'

I look over my shoulder before the hangar door blocks them from view. Cassie sits on Mary's shoulders, waving with both arms. Mary's hands hook around Cassie's ankles, feet spread wide to keep upright. I blow them a kiss, one each, then follow the men into the darkness, my heart in close pursuit.

*

The shuttle hatch closes with a sigh as the airlock engages and I take my seat behind the bridge controls.

'Captain,' says Michael, a mix of terror and excitement in his eyes. 'Good luck.'

It still feels weird to be called 'Captain', as if I'm an imposter, a stowaway who snuck into the real captain's clothes when she wasn't looking.

'Come on, Michael. You've been calling me Ava *outside* the ship, call me Ava *inside* the ship. You're putting me on edge.'

I give our navigation officer a wink and turn to address the rest of the crew, turning on the intercom so those on different levels can hear too, then I clap my hands together once.

'Ladies and Gentlemen. I am trusting each and every one of you with my life, and each and every one of you must trust the same of each other. We are all going to be a long way from our families for a while, so we must act as one together. Please keep sibling rivalry to a minimum.' A few nervous chuckles around the room. 'We've trained for this a thousand times and more. We will do exactly what we did in simulations over and over, but with no more red marks around our eyes from the VR goggles. This is it. This is what we've been working for. We are pioneers, paving the way to the future, and our future is up there.'

I point to the sky, and watch as nodding heads follow my indication.

'All crew to launch positions.' I touch the communication link on my temple. 'Control, we are ready for launch.'

The countdown begins, each number rattling through our collective heads like pennies in a vacuum cleaner. I don't know why they still do it now everything's powered by flux distribution. Tradition I suppose, or just a way to build tension. There's no earth-shattering engine engagement anymore, or even any fire, just a distortion in the air. Much less spectacular to watch, but much more efficient, less likely to accelerate global warming, and with such small waste production, it causes barely more pollution than a half hour commute. Still, the countdown continues, numbers decreasing in size, collective nausea increasing in intensity, until,

'T- minus one...'

'Maya, engage propulsion,' I say, checking my standing straps one last time. 'Anand, monitor our stabilisers, compensate for thirty knot wind by south, south west and reduce steadily until we clear Stratos. Okay everyone, see you in space.'

Flux distributors make a sound like a huge groan tube, those plastic toys around when my grandparents were children. It's as if it's all too much effort, but they're reliable nonetheless. We rock a little before the stabilisers find their footing, crew staggering slightly to the left as if choreographed, despite all being well-fastened.

Stomachs in mouths, we float steadily towards the outer reaches of our atmosphere, the thought itself asphyxiating, the knowledge as we pass the last few particles of oxygen and all we have to rely on are the cannisters stored on board. Breaching the blue, we call it, when colour fades to black and all you see is stars – the same experience when your body runs out of air.

'PsuedoGrav engaged,' says Corrine. 'The seatbelt sign has now been switched off.'

A few more chuckles and exasperated moans now as the tension slides away.

'Well done, all,' I say.

Cheers across the bridge and through the monitors from control and from the engineers beneath us.

'We're closing in on Safe Space,' says Anand.

'Okay. Michael, are the coordinates programmed for our test jump?'

'They're in.'

'Okay, is everyone ready?' Nervous nods from all directions. 'Give us another countdown then, Anand. Who doesn't love a good countdown?'

On zero, I press the two buttons and Corrine pulls the lever which propels us faster than anyone has ever been. Stars blur into lines, then to blank space through the panoramic quartz windows surrounding us. Time seems to slow, though what is time without the Earth and sun to relate it to. The jump takes less than a second, and a glimpse through the glass at the rear shows us just how far we've travelled.

A chorus of gasps with subtle tones of relief and wonder permeate our manufactured air.

'It's barely the size of a marble,' says Corrinne, brushing her dark hair away from her face. 'Amazing.'

It takes a while for the awe to settle, for us to remember why we're here, for us to come to terms with how far we are from home.

'Well, we survived,' I say. 'Not a bad start.'

More cheers from the speakers, a delay now as the communication laser takes longer to reach Earth.

'Congratulations, Captain.' The voice of General Giordano.

'Thank you. Now, Michael. Second coordinate series, input please – checks by Anand and Nia. System control, identify hazards on path to our next destination, cross-reference with satellite information and laser interference. Corrinne, please highlight any potential hazards on system control screen and bring them to me. Everyone else, let's go find us some alien bugs.'

*

A high-pitched squeal puts my brain in a headlock and squishes all the juices out.

'What the hell is that?' screams someone who's voice is carried away on the noise.

'Distress signal,' I shout. 'Why is it so loud?'

'Sorry,' says Nia, frantically tapping on screens as the squeal fades to tinnitus. 'Two communication channels opened at once.'

'I'm having your powdered masala later,' says Michael, his usually tanned face drained of all colour. 'And that's only a down payment on my compensation. Jesus, my ears feel like they're being plucked from my head.'

'Jesus won't hear you from here,' I say. 'And neither can I for that matter. So, was that a distress signal, or just interference?'

'It's definitely a distress signal,' says Nia. 'It's bordering on that orbit belt you can see in the distance.'

She points through the window at a large red planet, not unlike Mars, but with a ring of rocks circling it like hungry sharks. Three moons lie a little further away, spinning on their own axes, one with a moon of its own.

'Can you see the ship?' I ask.

'No. Must be on the other side.'

'How much flux reserve do we have, Clara?'

'Enough for a short detour,' she says. 'But whoever it is will have to stay onboard until we've finished.'

'Of course,' I say. 'We can't afford a trip back home. Michael, set coordinates to just past that red globe over there. Use laser targeting, it'll be quicker. Do we know of any crews due this end of the galaxy at the moment?'

'Departure records say there were two long-term flights in this quadrant about a week ago. One French, one Chinese. Neither have distress notes on the system, and neither should have been this far out anyway. Could it be a reflection?'

'Possible,' says Nia. 'But unlikely. Any reflections should be between the ship and Earth, not further out.'

'We'll find out soon,' I say.

The red planet looms over us, even from such a distance. What look like dust clouds swirl on its atmospheric surface, hiding anything beneath. The shark rocks swim in perfect circles around their prey. Occasionally one breaks free and plummets into the mist below, its burning carcass vanishing before impact.

'We should keep a safe distance,' says Michael, still wiggling a finger in his ear, opening and closing his mouth like a suffocating fish. 'Latch onto that moon's orbit.'

'Good idea,' I say, holding back that it was the obvious option.

A blinding flash of orange and red buffets the ship like a wave, stabilisers saving us from smashing into the moon.

'Solar flare,' says Nia. 'Shouldn't cause us any major problems. Any craft without flux distribution could struggle though. This system's sun is dying.'

Despite our proximity to the star, and solar protection screening set so low, the light isn't blinding. Just a warm tide reaches us with each of the smaller flares, like standing close to a bonfire in November. A swarm of darkness rests in front, a black hole, a shield of anti-matter.

'Could that be why?' I say, pointing at the cyclical void. 'This star isn't dying. It's being killed.'

*

As we drift alongside our moon companion, our frozen friend of revolving rock, the red planet is all we can see from port side. Its star now sits directly ahead, edges blurred by storms of fire, siphoned like oil from a broken engine.

'There!' shouts Anand, eye sockets glued to the electroscope. He passes it to me, careful not to alter its angle. 'See them?'

'Jesus,' I say.

'He won't hear you from here,' says Michael.

I ignore him. 'It's split into three pieces, maybe two salvageable. Only one with any possible survivors, I'm certain of that. What the hell were they doing out here, and so close to that hole as well? Do you think you can get us in there, Anand?'

'Without killing us all in the process, you mean?'

'Ideally'

'It's possible.'

'What are you thinking?'

'I can programme the stabilisers to focus in four different directions. They're sitting just on the edge, right? If we can get close enough, I can lock each stabiliser towards an asteroid in the belt. It may be able to hold us in stasis for long enough to reach them. Someone's going to have to walk the rest of the way.'

'Walk in an asteroid belt, are you out of your fucking mind?' says Michael.

'Can you see any other way?' I ask.

'We could stabilise outside of the field, join orbit without entering the belt itself. How long is our sample collector, Kai?'

'Eighty-two feet.'

'Why are you telling me in feet? Were you born in the two-thousands?'

'About twenty-five metres.'

'There's your answer. Pick them off the belt like a delicious plate of sushi.'

'Aren't you vegan?' says Kai.

'Avocado sushi. Does it matter? Just don't go walking when you don't have to. It's an unnecessary risk.'

'Captain?' says Anand, filtering into my contemplation.

'We'll need a bigger claw than a sample collection arm,' I say. 'But I agree, walking in the belt would put us in too much danger.' I hold the intercom button. 'Sakura, please can you come up to the bridge? We have an engineering issue that needs resolving.'

*

The claw won't win any awards for stylish design, it looks more like a child has been given free reign over a life-sized mechano set. There are struts welded onto other struts at awkward angles, bent sheet metal protecting reinforced hydraulics and sharp edges that could slice off an arm if caught at the wrong point. What more can we ask for from four hours work?

'Will it hold?' I ask.

'It'll hold that orbiter, but not much else. And not for long either,' says Sakura, rubbing her eyes free of ash as she frees herself from the welding mask.

'Is there anything more that could be done to strengthen it?'

'Not with the materials we have on board. We're not set up for this kind of work.'

'Okay. Let's get started then. Michael. Anand. Maya. Get us as close as you can to that ship.'

The red giant swells, dust clouds almost hypnotic in their motion. Static electricity leaps between gritty spirals, beautiful and threatening in equal measure. This is not a planet to visit on holiday. There will be no research here.

'Easy,' says Michael. 'Easy. Easy.'

'I'm being easy,' says Anand, sweat trickling down the side of his face.

A small, rogue, shark rock scrapes against the hull of the ship, escaping into the unending dark.

'Easy,' says Michael again.

'Stasis held.'

'Can you see any movement in there, Ava?' asks Nia.

'Nothing. Their electrical systems are down. They must be in reserve; the only output is the signal. No mutual communication pathway can be created. Ready the claw. Let's get out of here as soon as we can.'

Other than Anand, who's eyes are firmly on stabiliser screens, all eyes are focused on the sample collector. A mist of carbon dioxide sprays with each movement and at each joint of the telescopic arm. Reaching down between rocks, hurtling around a planet at differing speeds, all of them at thousands of kilo-metres per hour, the claw locks onto its target. It scrapes along the aluminium shell, so delicate under its bulky appendages, despite the rubber feet attached to the tips.

Please don't breach. Please don't breach.

'We're locked,' says Sakura. 'I'll start withdrawing now.'

'Wait,' says Anand. 'I need to adjust the…'

The ship shakes as if struck by lightning, twisting away from the red beast and its belt too fast to control.

'Solar flare!' More than one voice.

Two asteroids spin towards us. One flies out into space as Anand deflects it with a well-timed blast from a stabiliser, the other strikes the central hinge of the claw, bending it out of shape as we spin further towards the sun. More shark rocks pummel into the side of the ship, barely scratching the quartz, but putting strain on the frames that hold it in place. It endures, but for how long? Two more into the claw, one at the base and another at its central hinge, bursting the hydraulics and sever-ing head from tail.

The helm of the stranded ship tears off like the top of a soft-boiled egg, its contents spilling out into the dark beyond and heading towards the sun.

'No. All those people!' shouts Michael, before his ribs hit the central console.

'Go with the spin,' I say. 'We can slow it down once we're out of orbit.'

'The force is too strong,' says Anand. 'We'll lose half of our shielding.'

'We'll lose it all if we fight it.'

Centrifugal force carries those not quick enough to strap in straight to the windows, spatters of blood staining them like cathedral glass before the emergency lighting kicks in.

'Drop us down!' I say, voice strained and tight.

'Down?'

'Just do it. We need to get beneath the field. More rocks are breaking off every second.'

Thrusters engage from above, forcing us into the abyss. Limp bodies hit the ceiling, the failed PsuedoGrav no longer able to keep them rooted.

'Okay. We're out of the worst,' I say, about to breach the blue. 'Get this spin controlled before I throw up.'

Small alterations slowly bring our wild spin down to a casual pirouette and finally into relative stasis.

'Medic?' shouts Nia. 'I can't see. Please help me, I can't see.'

'The medics are both down.' A man's voice. The ringing in my head's too loud to tell who.

'All who are able, come to the bridge,' I say through the intercom. 'All with higher than first aid training, help who you can. Prioritise those with head wounds or breathing difficulties. All other able bodies, search the other levels for those who need help. Bring them here.'

'Where are all the people?' says Michael, electroscope cradled in bloodied hands. 'There's nothing but metal. Metal and plastic. Where are they? Did we just do that for a fucking junk ship?'

'What do you mean?'

'There's no one there. Look.'

I take the scope, adjust the lens to compensate for the bright light now coming from the dying star. The star that nearly killed us all.

'Maybe they're still in there. Maybe they held on.'

'All of them, Ava?'

'Well, we don't know how many were left.'

Beyond the debris, the star shines brighter still. I tap the settings to give us further shielding.

'The black hole. It's growing,' I say, not sure whether to believe myself. *Did I hit my head as well?* 'How is this possible? Expansion takes years and...'

An image sits at the centre of the hole. A woman on a cobbled street. She's holding her stomach, blood soaking her clothes and the stone beneath her. Something shimmers in the air around her, like gold leaf or fragments of glass. This woman, this dying woman, looks just like me, only younger. It's like watching myself on camera. But she isn't me. She's someone else, yet she feels so familiar.

Who are you?

Something glimmering off to the right, catches my eye like the flash of a fish in a lake. A dark figure grows as the hole contracts. Sharp edges like a polished blade, black screens like devil's eyes and grates below that smile at me, taunt me, as if it knows the answer to my question. The sun isn't fighting with the hole. They're using it. They must be harnessing the energy, somehow.

'A ship. Another ship. It's... It's not one of ours.'

'Not one of ours, what are you on about?' says Michael.

'It's not from Earth. The distress signal, it wasn't distress at all.'

I pull away from the scope as the floating demon comes into view, cries from the crew all merging into one collective wail of something darker than fear.

I'm sorry, Mary. I'm sorry, Cassie.

'It was bait.'

***

DESCEND

The god of thunder claps his hands and lightning cleaves the sky in two.

Another rock splits and crumbles, crashing somewhere below, out of sight, but firmly lodged in mind. They say don't look down, but with waves charging like bulls against the roughed, granite surface I'm clinging to, not looking down is an impossible task. Either way, should the next hold prove evasive, my fate will be set in stone.

Somewhere beneath this narrow ledge, lies instant death at best, or at worst, a slow, drawn-out meeting with my own mortality. I cling like a baby monkey clings to its mother, but if the mother were made of sandpaper and the baby's fingers of overripe fruit. Skin peels, and nails splinter with each crevice I dig them into. Bleeding toes frozen inside curved shoes try to wrap anything they can find: sharp, blunt, serrated. Adrenaline squeezes each beat from my heart quicker than the last, propelling me onwards.

The storm drifts closer. Its pressure fills my ears, flattening my optimism onto its back, securing it in place like pins through butterfly wings. If I'm not off this cliff soon, if solid ground isn't just around that corner...

My body will never be found.

*

Voices circle like vultures overhead. They know I'm here, just not where. More guards pulled from sleep, posted as reinforcements. They know who I am; they've heard the stories. Footsteps on stone floor, rifle checks: cartridges ejected and reinserted, levers pulled, bullets fed into chambers. It's a small army.

But so am I.

I retie my hair, tuck it into the back of my top and put on the beanie hat I had folded up in my pocket, black. Lifting the grate, I slash through the thick leather of the first guard's boot, feel his Achilles tendon snap and withdraw. He hops then falls with a grunt and a 'What the f...'. I finish the job before he makes too much noise, dragging him under the floor with me. He'll start to smell in a day or two. I'll be long gone by then.

The handle moves, but the door doesn't budge. Locked from the outside, so no one should be behind it. The lock's old. To be expected in a building like this. I press my ear against the thick oak, then slide across to the gap between the door and its frame. A whirring sound, electronic. The relay - just where she said it'd be. Listed building needs a relay system, no permission for any structural changes.

And with no relay. There's no power.

Footsteps behind: stone, rug, stone again. He's close. I slip behind a bookshelf, shadow not quite wide enough to hide me fully.

'Naz?' he says, voice coarse like thirty a day. 'Naz, are you in here?'

His gun enters the room before he does, pointing ahead, shaking with a lack of experience. He's robotic in his gait, scanning the room like he has a set movement pattern he can't deviate from. I slam the heel of my palm upwards into the butt of the gun, following through into his chin. The knife slips into his neck like a plane through a cloud and I direct his fall towards the grate to save time, roll him in to meet his friend.

Old locks can be picked with even the most basic of skill and the correct kind of pick. Half diamond for this one, three clicks and in. I close the door behind me after mopping up the blood with the guard's own jacket. Not perfect, but it won't matter when the lights are out.

The soft whirring of the relay's fans disguise the crashing of waves in the darkness outside. A small window, glazed but with the remnants of three old, iron bars, allows a sliver of quickly evaporating moonlight into the room, barely distinguishable from the flickering, electronic glow. Bundles of wires, linked with cable ties, snake around the machines. This is more than just a relay.

It's a server room.

*

Thunder rattles my chest like a baby with a toy, but masks the sound of my drill; a little more force to secure the bolts on the overhang. Rain, like droplets of ice, swirl up and under the cliff face as the storm draws over, its roars deterrents to anyone with any sense. I clutch a crimp hold, defiance muttered in the form of obscenities into the wind and down to the rocks below, looking ever sharper.

Toes slip, as does my heart, a strong gust nearly stripping me from the cliff face. I kick up in reflex, hard, chipping away at a disintegrating ledge. It slips again, through the falling rubble, fingers losing strength. Twisting, contorting, toes searching for anything they can find and finally settling in line with my shoulder. Straddling the rock in a dubious game of inverted twister, right hand blue, left hand blue as the bitter cold chews through the flesh and into the bone beneath. The wind spins the dial again, and I have no choice but to move.

Hooking a leg around my elbow, I hang in a figure-four, or a pretzel, depending on the angle. A long reach with the opposite arm to the next hold spreads me open like a kite, so tempting for the wind as it tries to rip me away to the sea once more. A small pocket, only big enough for three fingertips, supports most of my weight, thumb free to grip a little lower on a jagged spine. Blood trickles across my knuckles, and runs into my sleeve, a reminder to slow my movements, calculate each with more care.

I untuck my looped leg, bracing as another gust threatens to finish my mission early. Pulling my chest closer to the surface, I twist and finally find a foot hold worth finding. With my toes and heel wedged, thunder rumbling like the belly of a giant beast and lightning forking in the water below, a crack, wide enough for a spring cam, reveals itself like a mirage in a frozen desert.

The final cam dangles from my belt, presenting itself for service. I rip it from its carabiner and swing my arm around and up into the granite, pull on the stem for tension and pray that it holds. It does. But the swing lifts my heel from its brittle shelf, dangling my foot above the tempestuous sea like a fish on a line.

The god of thunder claps yet again, as if applauding the reaper on her catch of the day.

*

It can't be this easy.

I follow each of the wire bundles in both directions to their source and destination. Nothing too suspicious. One or two feed out through the wall in odd positions, could be the alarm system, could be a botch job for the Wi-Fi. I run my circuit tester across them. Dead, just dead wires with no link.

It can't be this easy.

Decryption USB plugged in via an adaptor, opposite end plugged into my gauntlet. A dim light illuminates my arm, code running across the screen as if in a hurry. With a loose ear on the radio I picked up from the first guard, volume turned down to the minimum, I skim through the code and pick out any files that could be of interest.

Video file. MP4. A little larger than the rest. I convert and run it using some old software not widely used and not widely known. Harder to detect.

A man, sitting in a chair, fills the screen on my forearm. Blank, grey walls. A bright light shining into his bloodied face. The sound's muted, but this is what we came for. *It has to be.* A dark figure steps towards the man, takes hold of his throat and squeezes. The man squirms in his seat, but his hands are bound behind the backrest and his feet to the legs of the chair. The back of the figure's other hand swipes across the man's face, blood spraying the wall to his left.

We knew the interrogations were happening. We knew they would be documented. But the brutality, no. Dark rooms with bright lights, some targeted threats maybe. This needs to be made public, for all to see. This is what our government is doing to people. Now, where are these prisoners being kept?

'We know you're in there.' A voice from beyond the door, smooth but strong.

Fuck. Silent alarm.

I play for time, stick the half diamond pick into the lock, twist, and leave it in place so a key won't work.

'Locking yourself in?' says the voice. 'You're just delaying the inevitable.'

It'll take quite some force to get through that solid door. I have a few minutes at least. Removing my gauntlet and laying it down, wire attached, I let it download as much as possible whilst I work on the exit route. I drag one of the least packed server shelves to the centre of the room with a swivelling motion, black, semi-circular lines drawn across the stone floor with the rubber feet.

The first shelf bows under my weight, so I use the edge of the next one, holding onto the bar to relieve some of the pressure. Third supports me well, and the fourth has no equipment on so I slide myself across it on my back, facing the window above.

A crash at the door as something slams into the wood.

'Again,' says the voice from before.

Another crash, but no signs of giving. Not yet.

Butterfly knife from the holster on my thigh, I jam the blade under the frame and into the crumbling stone beneath, twisting and prying. Sparks from the stone as I saw at the sealant, blunting my brand-new knife after only two uses. What a waste.

Another crash. Splintering sound. Not long now.

The window pivots slightly, then wedges itself into a different position, corner dug into the edge of the recess. I slam a palm into the glass nearest the same corner and get nowhere. Instead, carving away at the sealant near the opposite side, I manage to slip a finger around, grating it on the rough surface, but clutching on the plastic.

Another crash. Metal on metal this time. They've realised they should be focusing their efforts on the locking mechanism. The handle budges, sticking further out into the room than it was. Any moment now.

A second finger slips in next to the first and I pull, skin pulling away, but window moving too. Palm placed on the opposite side. Knife held between teeth. Slowly. Slowly, it comes, rubber seal folding back and giving, plastic splitting and...

One last blow of the ram and the door handle flies into the room, skidding across the floor and under the shelf my gauntlet sits on.

'There you are.'

*

Both hands wrapped around the spring cam, cold steel not welcoming to even colder hands. Waves lick at my dangling feet as if hungry for flesh, spray reaching me now, droplets gathering on my clothes before falling back down, giving the sea a taste of what's to come.

Water seeps between my palms and the cam, stealing away any scraps of friction I'd managed to trap. I close my eyes and clench my teeth, willing some grip back into my failing fingers. So tired. So, so tired.

Bit by bit I slide towards the end of the cam – the end of me. Bit by bit, the sea widens its dusky maw – taunting grin morphing into gaping chasm, waves clashing like teeth. Little finger, left hand, loosens, ring finger follows as thunder shakes another rock down from above, scraping at my cheek as it falls.

If I die, so does she. So do countless others.

So, fucking climb.

Right index finger, slides up, hooks around the cam's axle and my thumb on the other side, nail slicing across sodden skin. Twist of the torso and a stretch of my left hand, grabbing higher up the main shaft. I swing my body back, then power forwards, kicking towards a shadow in the rock. No hold. Another swing, another shadow. Toes find a shelf and stick, enough to lift the other leg slowly and wedge it between two small stalactites lit up by a flash from the sky.

My watch buzzes. Alarm. Not long now.

Only a few more moves until the standing ledge. The rest will be easy, if I can just warm up my hands.

*

Leaning back, arcing over the edge of the server's shelf I throw the window at the owner of the voice, a tall man with tanned skin and dyed blonde hair. It hits his eyebrow, blood spattering down his fresh, white shirt. I take the knife from between my teeth and throw that too. It slices into the throat of the next guard, arterial spray decorating his leader who pushes him back and dives towards me in one swift motion.

I grip hard then tip the shelves on top of him, knocking him over and the gauntlet under the server, still downloading. As long as they focus on me, we'll get the data. Twisting my elbows outwards, I lever myself through the small window, shoulders barely slim enough to fit.

'Get outside,' he shouts as lightning forks into the sea beyond the cliffs.

He better be ready.

Rain swirls, lashing like whips from every angle, soaking me in seconds. I swivel the carabiner across my belt, ready to attach. Thunder claps and I duck as if being shot at, then a shot rings from an invisible shooter and I duck as if cowering from the thunder. The bullet hits something in the distance. *They can't see. It's too dark.* All but when the lightning strikes.

I slide across terracotta tiles, using their furrows to guide me down towards the guttering. A loose pin catches my heel, forcing a tile free. Spinning one-eighty, head towards the edge, another pin catching my waist and slicing into the skin. I skid faster and faster, tiles too slick with water to catch myself. The wind howls as I do, slamming my palm into the roof, flipping my feet back towards the end of the roof. One heel hits the guttering with a crack, slipping over and into naked air. The other jabs in and buckles my knee, twisting it outwards with a snap at the front and side.

A boar-like grunt runs from my lungs, along with my breath, as an elbow crashes into the gutter, legs flailing below, useless with the wall too far to reach. Elbow collapses onto forearm, fingers spread wide, wrist grating on the rough metal struts. Lightning illuminates the downpipe like a beacon of hope and I shuffle towards it, right forearm in and left hand gripping the outside ledge.

Wrapping my feet as best I can around the downpipe, I slither towards the ground, slowing at each bracket to keep all of my fingers. Earth meets grateful feet with a thud as a security light glares, its beam cutting a wedge into the darkness. A bullet strikes the wall next to my head with a violent shattering of old stone.

Crouch. Run.

The beam of light follows me like an attack hound. In the lull between thunder and screeching wind, rifle shots echo from the clouds. I zigzag, sporadically, just as I was taught.

An unpredictable target is more evasive than a small one.

But luck is a finite substance.

A bullet grazes my cheek as I look back, taking a layer or two of skin with it. A second rips a hole into my top and penetrates a rock just ahead. The third hits home. As if a screwdriver has been ploughed into it, my thigh jerks and folds my leg in two, muscles spasming. I hop twice on my other leg then fall in a heap, bullets hitting the ground just behind.

The edge of the world is just there. If I make it to the edge, I make it home.

Dragging myself to my feet, leaning into the wind, I hobble as fast as possible. Carabiner in position, rope at the edge already knotted. I slip it through the screw gate, no time to secure it.

'Hey!'

His voice reaches through the din and turns me back. The man, only his silhouette visible against the bright security light. I smile and step backwards towards the edge, all but my toes already over. A flash lights his face for a moment, eyes wild like the night sky. It strikes like a punch to the chest and I fall towards the sea.

*

Back resting against the rough wall, hands spread but body compacted to avoid the brunt of the wind. I skirt across the narrow shelf, unravelling rope as I go, ground expanding until my legs dissolve into bands of wet liquorice and splay beneath me. Safe.

Sa*fer*.

Another buzz of watch against wrist. I roll onto my front, lever myself onto elbows, coil of rope resting beneath my hip, tilting me.

Download Complete!

Transfer Complete!

The two messages sit above their individual loading bars. She did it. She'll be on her way, ready when the third message comes through.

Thunder still roars overhead, but the waves are slowing now, not so much crashing as lapping at the rocks. Or maybe that's just perspective now I'm not suspended above them. Walking along the verge of this small ridge, I pray Thor spared more mercy for our boat than he did for me on the climb. We tied it fast with drilled bolts to secure it, galvanised hull with a thick rubber fender to ward off the rocks. I shine my torch down towards its little alcove, half on the beach, half off. Just where we left it, and intact too. Something went right at least. With warmth slowly snaking its way back into my fingers, I sit next to the rope and wait for her signal.

I scroll through the transferred files until I find one she flagged. The only one. The tiny screen, obscured by rain, is almost impossible to see. I turn up the volume in my Bluetooth earpiece, seated so deep it blocks out the outside world.

'Tell us what you know about fate,' says a man behind the camera.

'I don't know what you mean.'

A crack and a groan.

'We know what you are.'

'Tell me,' says the second voice, a gurgle. 'What am I?'

'You're...'

The man starts but his voice pops and fizzes like a dying

circuit. He coughs, wheezes, struggles to draw breath. Something snaps.

'Go on,' says the second voice, spitting a glob of blood onto the floor. 'Spit it out.'

'That's enough, Oliver.' A third voice. A woman, young sounding, but thick with tones of authority. 'If you won't tell us willingly, we'll…'

A scream pierces my ear and I slap my watch to stop the recording. A rubbing sound replaces it, or slipping, something moving. I lean out onto my outstretched hand and the rope coils around my wrist like a snare, snatching my arm out from under me.

I hook a weary leg around a boulder, sharp edged and cutting. I pull back with my wrist, catching the rope with my other hand. It jolts as if snagged, then releases again sliding through my grip and across the taut tendons it wraps, burning through the skin like flame through paper. I twist my tethered hand and catch the rope in both palms, gripping with all of my strength. It snags again, then releases, but this time I'm ready.

A shadow swings across the gorge, arms and legs draped, back arched like a crescent moon, falling.

'No!' I shout into the storm.

I lurch to my feet, body trembling, shaking with the effort to slow her fall. Another cam gives, force too strong for them to hold, but each jolt contorting her body even more. I jam my heels into the earth, lean back with all my weight, pull with everything I have, but still she falls, disappearing into shadow again as the overhang swallows her limp form.

It's the only way.

I jump from the ridge, down towards sea level, down towards the rocks like spines jutting from the earth. Another jolt as I drop, gathering speed now, aiming between the sharpest of the stony spikes, for the gritty sand that won't impale me. Breath held. Heart stopped. Bracing for the inevitable blow and the pain that follows.

But it slows, her weight catching mine, no more jolting, just smooth descent as she rises back towards the overhang, swaying gently as another bolt strikes in the distance. Saved by the same spring cam that saved me.

I land on a rock, but softly enough to slow and walk down its edge. Taking the torch from my pocket, I aim it at her but pause with a finger resting on the button. A different light, an artificial one, shines down from the cliff above. They won't see her from there, just the remnants of the storm in the sea and the promise that she won't have survived. A promise that won't be kept.

It only takes a couple of minutes for them to give up their search, so I work my way around to the boat, rope now securely fastened to my belaying harness. No sign of movement yet. I need to be quick.

With one hand steering the boat and the other releasing the rope in stages, I work my way towards her. Once I'm directly beneath, I tether the boat to a stalagmite protruding from the water, keeping the engine running in case of a swell.

Slow now. Slow.

Ava floats down into my lap like a drowned angel, hair plastered across her pale cheeks, soaked through and shivering. *Shivering like a living person.* She coughs, and groans, grabbing hold of her chest. A hole ripped through her top, right through to the Kevlar.

'You were right about the vest,' she says, coughing again, nestling into my neck. 'I wish we'd got the bottoms too though. This really, bloody hurts.'

She bends up her knee and wraps her hands around the back of her thigh.

'What happened?' I ask.

'Don't worry, it'll be fine. Did we get everything?'

I wrap her in my arms, try to squeeze the pain from her, try to take some of it on myself.

'We got it,' I say. 'We have everything we need.'

***

NUCLEUS

A loud bang at the door makes me jump. Two more wrap dread around fear like an unwanted gift and force it deep into the pit of my stomach.

It's still here.

'What are you doing in there, Oliver?'

Dad's voice is booming. I feel it in my chest, like a phone ringing inside.

'Nothing,' I say, cradling the shards in my bleeding hands, straining to not let my voice quiver.

His knock made me grip. The glass sticks out of my palm like the spines on the back of a stegosaurus. It was my favourite dinosaur. Not anymore.

'It doesn't sound like nothing. Unlock the door, now.'

'Okay. Coming.'

I pull two of the three pieces from my palm with a wince and gritted teeth. The third is curved; the base of mum's vase. It tugs at the skin as it comes, which tugs a whimper from my mouth.

'What was that?' asks Dad. 'I'm coming in. Get away from the door.'

With no time to move, the swinging door meets my forehead with a crack and a white flash splits the room.

The power swells. It's growing.

*

I was eight and a half when I first felt the energy. It swirled and buffeted like a gale around my guts, just beneath the skin. It made me feel sick at first. I had a day off school with a temperature. That's normal, apparently. I've done some research. It's the body's way of helping it to "bed in". My immune system had to realise it wasn't an enemy, but a friend.

The first time I really noticed it came just after, maybe a week or two. I was walking past my bedside table, the same way I did every day before that, but this time was different. The glass with water I had for bed was vibrating, ripples across the water. I squeezed my hand into a fist and it stopped. I opened it again and the ripples came back. The window was closed and so was the door. So, what was it?

I tested it with other glasses scattered around my room, but this was the one that worked. For the next ten minutes the ripples came and went whenever I asked them to. Ten minutes later and they were gone, no matter how hard I tried. The power left a metallic taste in my mouth, like when you bite your tongue. And it drained me. Not like after a game of football, but like someone had taken all of the sugar from my blood and left me only with salt. My science teacher told me what happens when we run out of sugar, so I crawled downstairs and crammed half a pot of Nutella into my mouth.

Dad wasn't happy. I was.

*

'I'm worried about him, Ava. I really am. He's acting even stranger than he was before.' I hold the phone with my cheek and shoulder, sliding my hands into the oven gloves, striped with baby pink and dotted with the burns of parental distraction.

Steam billows from the cooker and coats my glasses. I wipe them with the gloves, but the water just streaks across.

'He's up in his room at the moment. God knows what he's

doing, probably having a séance or making a Ouija board or something. I feel like he needs more help than he's getting.'

I flip over the chicken nuggets with a half-melted, plastic spatula and shuffle the chips to unstick them from the baking tray. One minute and thirty seconds on the microwave to get the beans going. Give them enough time to cool down this time.

'No. He hasn't done anything like that. Not to my knowledge anyway, but I wouldn't put it past him.' I lower my voice to a whisper, despite him being well out of earshot. 'To be honest, he's creeping me out a bit. It's not like I'm scared or anything like that, but the way he talks now, he's like an old man in a child's body.'

Timer reset for ten minutes.

'Have you ever felt like this with your kids before? Please tell me it's not just me... oh, it is? Well in that case, do you know anyone I could speak to?'

I take the phone from my shoulder and straighten up my neck with a crack. The oven glove will be earning another brown spot having edged its way into the corner of the cooker door. With a thumb on one temple and an index finger on an eyebrow I squeeze my face and add to the wrinkles that are deepening with each passing day.

'Can you give me their number?' A crash from upstairs. 'I'll have to call you back, Ava.'

The phone cracks as I slam it down on the worktop, thumb squeezing the button to hang up. Stairs two at a time using the bannister for leverage, I'm at the top in under ten seconds.

'What are you doing in there, Oliver?' I say, three hard bangs on the door with the side of my fist.

'Nothing,' he says, as always.

'It doesn't sound like nothing. Unlock the door, now.'

It sounds like rats in the walls as he scrabbles around inside, trying to hide something, no doubt. I knew that lock was a bad idea when we bought it for him.

'Okay, coming,' he says.

Leaning against the door frame and tapping my foot on the floor, I slow my breathing. *When was the last time I moved that fast?* A whimper like a hungry puppy. He's hurting himself, just like Ava said.

'What was that?' I ask. 'I'm coming in. Get away from the door.'

Two steps back and one leap forward, heel pounding into wood, latch ripping from the frame taking splinters and chipped gloss paint with it. The door swings into the room, stopping too soon. A grunt and another bang as he hits the floor.

'Oh no.'

He can't hear me. His eyes are open with no focus, staring at the ceiling. Glass lies all around him, one hand clenched and bleeding between the fingers. A purple stain spreads across his forehead, bulging at the centre, split in half by the groove left from the impact. *I'm a terrible father.* Eyes glare at me from the walls as I pick him up and cradle him in my arms: punk bands and skateboarders and rock climbers all disgusted, all witnesses to my failure.

Tears gather, blurring my vision as I wrap his convulsing body in his winter coat and open the front door. *What have I done? What have I done?* He shakes and shakes like something inside him is trying to break its way out. A beeping sound creeps into the back of my mind just before the door closes, like I'm forgetting something. A reminder stolen by the wind. It doesn't matter.

Not now.

*

I wake up to mum's smile, as I often do. It sways gently from side to side.

It starts out nice, like a dream I don't want to wake up from. I reach out to hold her, like I used to, before. White bubbles ooze from her lips. Her eyes bulge like a shocked cartoon, red and sore and dying. Her jaw juts forwards as the rope slides higher, forcing her tongue between her teeth, somehow still smiling. Her body is stiff and scratches snake from her chin to her neck as if she's had a fight with Mrs Rampton's cat.

I used to get scared. When she first visited, I cried for hours, didn't sleep for weeks. Now though, I know. She's the source of my power. Her clenched fists reach out towards me and I take hold of them, prise her nails from her palms and absorb what she has to give. This is the big one. She knows she can trust me now. It's time to move on.

Eyes drift. A shutter falls down between us and when it withdraws, she's gone.

'Oliver, are you okay?'

Dad's eyebrows are close together, almost touching, like kissing caterpillars. His glasses slip down his nose as he leans over me.

'Of course, I'm okay.'

He doesn't understand. I don't think he ever will.

'You're in hospital, Oliver. You had a knock to the head. It was my fault. I'm sorry. I'm so sorry I hurt you.' He hugs me like he thinks I'm going to break.

'I know what you did, Dad, and I forgive you. It doesn't hurt. Not much.' I touch the corner of my forehead, covered in bandage. 'My hand feels worse. I'm sorry about mum's vase.'

'It's fine. And if you need any more painkillers, just tell me or the nurse, okay?'

'I will.' I won't. I don't want to get sleepy again. Sleepy drains the power. Sleepy sends mum away again. 'How long was I asleep for, about ninety-five minutes?'

'Erm.' He looks at his watch. 'About an hour and a half, yeah. How did you know?'

'It's easy for me.' I trace the edges of the bandage on my hand. I can't open it properly. That must be why I can't feel the energy working. 'I'm hungry.'

Dad's face drops like the coin I threw from that balcony in Spain. He didn't like it when I did that either. He doesn't like a lot of what I do since mum died. He used to smile before. Now he just looks lost.

'I've got to go for a while,' he says. 'I'll ask one of the nurses to bring you something.'

He runs towards the door until he gets asked to stop. Then he walks quickly with occasional skips, like a malfunctioning robot. I only told him I was hungry to remind him to eat himself. I'm not hungry at all. In fact, I feel a bit queasy, like the first time I saw her smile.

I just hope he gets back in time to save the house.

*

My knees hit the floor, instantly sodden from the wet grass.

Everything lost but the car and the clothes I'm wearing. Mouths of flame gape from the roof up towards the sky like hungry chicks, their mother hidden somewhere in the smoke above.

Two hands grip my shoulders and pull me back as a window bursts and more fire rushes out into the air. I pull away, towards the house, crawling on all fours. *Take me with you. Oliver will be better off without me.*

Four more hands grab at my chest and waist, anchoring me to the ground then sliding me towards the road. Voices swirl in my head, but the sirens and the flames and the alarms are all too much to process. I close my eyes and turn inwards, chest heaving with every crying breath.

All of her clothes, her soft toys, her makeup and hair products. Her artwork and screenplays, all exactly where she left them for so long. Her oven gloves she refused to let me replace. The pictures, nothing digital, all print to make them mean more, she said. They did mean more. They meant *so* much more.

There will be nothing left but a shell filled with ashes. The home we built for ourselves, for Oliver, will be nothing but a memory, tarnishing a little more with every passing moment.

*

'It's not your fault, Dad,' he says, stroking my hair like I do for him when he's upset.

'Of course, it is,' I say. 'But, don't worry. We'll be fine. We'll always be fine.'

'It was Mum.' He lays a hand on each of my cheeks and tilts my head up, away from the scratchy hospital blanket. 'She didn't want us to live there anymore. She wants us to move on.'

I swallow, but all of the moisture has been sapped away. The words come out in rasps. 'What do you mean?'

'I told you before about my powers, didn't I?' He waits. I nod. 'They're from Mum. They've always been from Mum. She visits me every time it happens.'

Stay calm. Act calm, at least.

'She visits?

'Well, it's not like she knocks on the door and asks to come in. She just hangs there, watching me, smiling. Then everything goes black for a few seconds and after that, something happens. Like with the vase.'

Hang. If any word pulls shivers up my spine, it's that one. Oh, Oliver. What do I say to a boy who thinks his dead mum's looking after him from beyond the grave? He won't believe me if I tell him it's not her, or he won't want to believe me.

'Don't worry about that at the moment, Oli. It's not your fault, or your mum's. You just get some rest and heal up. Then we'll talk about what happens next. I'm going to speak to the doctor now, okay?'

With the blanket pulled up to his chin, Oliver closes his eyes and pretends to fall asleep. The doctor pokes his head around the door, white hair ruffled like goose feathers.

'Are you ready?'

He takes me to an office attached to the ward and asks a nurse to leave, closing the door behind her with a click. The smell of disinfectant is masked by the intense aroma of strong coffee as the doctor holds the white mug out towards me. I take it with a thankful nod and wrap it with my fingers, letting the warmth percolate through my skin.

'Thank you,' I say. 'So, have you got any news?'

'The CT scan has come back clear, no signs of bleeding on the brain,' he says, as if a but is on the way. 'But, when you were speaking to the police yesterday, he was talking to me about these special powers of his. He told me he sees flashing lights or all the lights go off or something along those lines. Has he ever mentioned this to you before?'

'A few years ago, he started talking about 'abilities', so it's nothing new if that's what you mean?'

A look of relief spreads across the doctor's face. 'Was there any inciting incident when he started talking about this?'

'His mother committed suicide when he was eight years old. It's had a big impact on him, on both of us. Look, is this relevant? Is my son going to be okay?'

'His physical injuries are generally superficial. He will make a full recovery, though he may have some scarring by his eye and on his hand and these may stretch as he grows. I will ask one of our nurses to speak to you about aftercare. My main worry is for his mental health. He has already had so much trauma in his life for someone so young, and now he's lost his home as well. His behaviour may well become more erratic before it improves. Has he ever had any help, following the death of your wife?'

'We weren't married.'

'Sorry. Your partner.' He looks down towards his pad of paper, pen poised.

'He's had counselling. It didn't last long. He had input from a child bereavement charity as well. They were great, but there was only so much they could do. With people he doesn't know, he usually acts so... normal. When it's just me and him, I don't know, he seems to turn into a different person. He just keeps on and on about his abilities and he seems to know things he shouldn't.'

His face stays pointed down as his eyes roll up to meet mine. 'What kind of things?'

'Oh, erm. For example, he knew that I was going to be late to pick him up from school once. He told one of his teachers exactly when I would arrive and what my reason would be. There's no way he could've found that out before I told him. And once, he brought me a specific screwdriver for a project I was working on at home. One I didn't even realise I owned and at exactly the time I needed it.'

'Coincidences?' he says, lingering on the final 's' sound.

'It happens too often for that. He can do things I can't fathom. Nothing like what he talks about, but he's not a *normal* boy. It's like he can read your mind or see the future or something. I know it can't be real, but I can't just ignore it or explain it away anymore.'

'You've been under a lot of pressure yourself, Mr Sanguine.'

'You're right. Maybe I'm just going mad. That's probably it. I'm going mad.'

'Mad may be a bit of a strong word. Tell you what, to ease the strain a little, I'm going to refer Oliver for some psychological tests and some further imaging to put your mind at ease.'

'That would be great,' I say. 'I'd really appreciate that. We both would. Will it be here at the hospital?'

'The imaging yes, we'll get that done as soon as a slot is available. For the testing, we usually say the therapeutic input should start as soon as a problem is identified. For this reason, we'll actually have to transfer him to another facility. It's a little way from here and, unfortunately, we can't let you visit him, for obvious reasons.'

'And what are the obvious reasons?'

'Sorry, Mr Sanguine. I do have a tendency of assuming people are aware of these systems when, of course, you are not part of the system yourself.'

He pauses and looks to the ceiling, as if searching for inspiration.

'It's Sanglin. So, what are they?' I ask again.

'People with delicate psychological conditions often take very little to be pushed into hysteria. I'm not talking about Oliver now, of course, but there are other children, and adults, in this facility who are extremely sensitive to change. To have visitors for every patient coming in and out willy-nilly on a daily basis would create carnage in such a fragile environment. I'm sure you can understand this. The success of the programme relies on a very specific, therapeutic milieu, so to speak.'

'Will Oliver be safe in this milieu?'

'Oh, yes. Safety is of the utmost importance, hence the restriction of visiting. Day leave may be permitted if it is deemed appropriate at the time of the request.'

'And how long would Oliver be expected to be in this "facility"?'

It makes sense to do this now, under a doctor's recommendation. I'll have a chance to find a new place to live and try to scrape together the tatters of our lives, all the while with Oliver getting professional help.

'There have been huge steps forward in the treatment of mental health conditions in recent years, so it will be a lot quicker than it would've been say, a decade ago.'

'So, how long?'

'It's impossible to say at this stage, but he appears to be in quite a good state considering what he's been through. I imagine he will be considered a good candidate for treatment and hopefully will not need to be there for too long.'

'Can you give me even a hint of a timescale? I agree, it sounds like a perfect opportunity for us, but I would like to know how long I won't be able to see my son for.'

'It's not really my area of expertise, sorry.' He cradles his bearded chin on a curled index finger and the knuckle of a thumb. 'How about this? I'll ask for a personal report as soon as the initial findings are gathered and, as soon as I hear, I'll let you know. They will be able to give us a length of stay prediction before his formal admission, as they need to do this for commissioning reasons anyway. If you think it will be too long, you can always withdraw him from the programme prior to commencement. How does that sound?'

'It sounds like a plan. I'll talk with Oliver. I'm not sure how happy he'll be about it, but I'm sure I can convince him.'

*

Waves crash against the cliff like they're trying to knock it down, like it's a door and they want something behind it. It's been a long time since I was properly scared and I don't like it. My hand's still bandaged and Mum hasn't been here for ages. *Where has she gone?* I need her now, more than I ever have.

'Okay. We're here. Everybody out.'

The brakes of the ambulance squeak and the two big men with dark clothes, who were sitting behind me, are out before the driver. The lady from the hospital opens an umbrella and runs into the headlight glare.

'Can you walk?' says a guard, sliding the side door open and letting the wind smack me in the face.

'Obviously he can walk, Naz. He's mental, not crippled.'

Mental? Dad said this was to help me get back to normal. Whatever that means. I told him I feel better than I ever have. He said that was the problem. But why is being happy a problem?

'You better hope he's not just mental or you'll have to get him to the auction house and I'll make sure you get put up in that hostel you had last time.' He sticks his tongue into the inside of his cheek with his fist in front of his mouth like he's holding a microphone. Then he pretends to bite the top off and spit it out on the ground. He turns to me. 'Come on, mate. Let's get you into the warm.'

It doesn't look warm. It looks dark, something straight out of a horror film. The only thing missing is the murder of crows flying in circles above. A murder is a weird collective term. I like it. Maybe they'll come when the wind calms down.

The old pipes that feed the shower gurgle and hiss as Naz turns an iron valve. The room smells damp before the water even gets there and it tastes funny when it gets in your mouth, like it's being pumped from a murky pond. I screw my eyes shut so it can't get in. I don't want to get blinded on my first day here.

Steam rises from the cold floor and fills the room. It reminds me of smoke, like what our house must have looked like from the inside, only not quite as hot. The bandage on my hand slips and slaps against my body as it moves, even though they told me to keep it dry. I pull back the sloppy fabric a bit to look at the scars, so I know what I have to live with from now on. My fingers open fine, but the skin on my palm stretches and splits around the threads holding it together. I don't cry, but my eyes want to.

A movement in the dark takes my attention. Like someone's pulling at the steam from both sides, it separates in the middle.

'Mum?' I say, the fear melting away, pouring towards the drain in a stream.

She swings like she always does, each movement creating a ripple in the water below, her flowing dress dripping into a foamy pool. My brain swells with her energy.

'You came back for me.' I open my hand wider, the pain no match for my joy. 'I knew you would.'

A water pipe bends and splits as that wonderful, metallic taste coats my tongue and my body starts to shake. I hold onto the moment for a second more, then let the darkness take over, excited to see what will happen while I'm gone.

*

Three days and still no word. He told me two, at most. I hope Oliver's okay.

The bald insurance guy's words drift around me like falling feathers as I stare at the top of his head, shading in the reflection of the setting sun with my mind. He snaps his folder shut and snaps me out of my hypnosis.

'So, as mentioned earlier, Sir, it appears we cannot provide any reimbursement due to the inconsistency of your policy details.'

'You what?'

'Your wife's name was on the documents, not yours. She, may she rest in peace, no longer lives here and therefore the policy is void.'

'But all of the other details are the same and the insurance has always been automatically renewed. Paper-free. I had no chance to make any changes. There has to be something you can do about this. I have a son.'

'I'm aware you have a son, Sir. But this is effectively fraud, and you are lucky we aren't informing the police, if I'm honest.'

'Get out,' I say, under my breath.

'Sorry, what did you say, Sir?' He leans towards me, over the cheap, scratched, hotel coffee table.

'I said, if you can't help me, if you're going to sit their lecturing me about fraud and telling me I'm lucky when my house has burned to the ground and my son's locked in some asylum somewhere, you can get out of this fucking room before I tear your scabby little tongue from that arsehole you call a mouth and stuff it somewhere you'd rather it not be fucking stuffed.'

'I will not tolerate being talked to like this.' He zips up his briefcase and rearranges his paisley tie.

'Well you best leave quick then because there's a lot more of that to come if you stay any longer you fucking little weasel. Now get out, because I am a man of my word and I promise you, in five minutes time you'll be crawling out of that door on two broken legs with this pen sticking out of your cheek.'

I hold the pen towards him, hand shaking as rage fills it. He walks to the door in pseudo-composure, but his footsteps quicken in the corridor and to a sprint before he makes it to the end.

I need to find out how Oliver is.

Phone in hand, I search the hospital's name on Chrome then call the number that comes up. A woman answers, the sound of pen on paper underneath the receiver reminding me to release the grip on mine.

'Hello, ward 9, Children's. Helen speaking.'

Lip firmly held between teeth, I force my heart to slow and my voice to steady. 'Hi, my son, Oliver Sanglin was in with you about three days ago. He was under Doctor... erm, sorry I can't remember his name.'

'Little Oli, yeah I remember him. What was your question?'

'I was waiting to hear back from the Doctor about how he's getting on at the mental health facility. He said he would get back to me by yesterday about the initial findings, but I think I'd rather just have him home and take my chances.'

'Mr Sanguine, is it?'

'Sanglin.'

'Oh, sorry. Mr Sanglin, let me just check his discharge letter to find out who dealt with him. I'm just going to put you on hold, is that okay?'

'No problem.'

A stinging in my neck feels closer to regret the more I rub. I should've tried to reason with that insurance vulture, maybe there was some way to negotiate with him. This isn't me. All this anger. This just isn't me. I need to calm down and think like a reasonable person again.

'Hi, Mr Sanguine?'

'Sanglin.'

'Sorry. The letter here says your son was discharged home. Our records say he left with his mother?'

'No, you've got that wrong. His mum died almost 5 years ago. Check again, please.'

She reads me our address, or what once was. She tells me three times what the letter says and assures me it's his. My heart drums off-beat and sweat trickles down my back.

'We even have his mother's signature on discharge because it was earlier than we'd originally agreed to. It says her name is Penny. Is that right?'

How do they have her name? They must have asked him. That's it, they must have asked him.

'Yes. That *was* her name. Where's my son, please? He's not with me and I'm the only family he has. Let me speak to the doctor, now.'

'If you don't have a name, I can't transfer you.'

'Oh, for fuck sake. He had white hair and a beard, a dusty pink shirt...'

'Please do not swear at me, Sir or I will hang up the phone. We don't have any doctors with white hair working here. The last one we did have retired about three years ago. Are you sure you're remembering correctly?'

'I'm sure. I'm positive. Find my son and tell me when you have.'

I tap the red button on the phone screen, silencing her wasted consolation. My head hits the back of the hard sofa with a thud. I do it again, and again trying to fight away the dread. It doesn't work.

The pain is just a momentary distraction, a harsh but preferable reality to dull this waking nightmare.

*

The nice lady from the hospital leads me downstairs into a room without windows. There's a white screen set up behind a table with a lamp on it. It looks like one of those terrorist videos they show on the news sometimes.

'What's this for?' I ask, pointing at a video camera on a stand. 'Am I going to be famous?'

She laughs, humouring me. Pretence solid, my reliable façade.

'No. Not famous as such. Have a seat,' she says, open hand towards the metal chair.

'It doesn't look very comfortable,' I say.

'Sit down.' A voice comes from the shadows and I do as I'm

told.

'Who's that?'

A dark figure moves into the fringes of the lamplight. His clothes are black, thick boots, thick gloves, heavy jacket and weird, ridged trousers with no pockets. A transparent mask covers his face, a white beard bordering his thin, straight lips.

'I remember you,' I say. 'You were at the hospital.'

The nice lady leaves the room and closes the door, locks it from the outside.

'You will ask no questions. You will only do as I say,' says the doctor. 'Now. Show me what you can do.'

Mum dangles from the ceiling, her toes in line with the doctor's waist. I spread my fingers wide, clenching my jaw at my hand's painful protests, and look to her for confirmation.

She smiles and so do I.

***

A LIBRARY OF THOUGHTS: PART ONE

Twelve

I slam the book closed, the story too close to reality, too close to home. I choke down the tears and smooth the lump in my throat, wayward thoughts pooling in the back of my mind, threatening to drown me. So much detail, each and every one stinging like a freshly salted wound. How could someone who knows nothing of me know me so well?

For days I search through the words, picking them apart like scraps from a bone for anything out of place, for something that doesn't belong. But everything belongs. Only subtleties and nuances are missing, as if my memories have been lost in translation, a foreign film with the same actors.

Half a bottle of whisky dulls the prickling sensation in my head, synapses bridging for the first time in years, recollections I'd rather not recollect. It can't be about me. It can't be.

And yet it is.

*

Oliver

Waves should put you to sleep, I think. Not me. They just drown out the screams when they're strong. It doesn't last forever like I wish it would. The screams get louder and the waves get quieter. Sometimes the thunder's nice though, and the rain against the bricks. They last longer when the storms come over the top of us. They help me sleep, and they've been getting louder recently.

I met a girl yesterday. She had black hair and a sad face. She told me she'd get us out of here if I gave her my pudding. I told her they don't give us any pudding, just the sloppy porridge that tastes like the sea. She told me she hears voices at night, that they're making a plan together, that I can come with them if I give her my pudding. But I didn't have any pudding, so I guess I'm staying here.

They're going to take me to the room again soon. They'll ask me to move things without touching them. I said I can only do it when people aren't watching and when I get really angry or scared. I don't like the room. Mum never comes with me anymore and I feel like a little boy again, not a grown-up. When she's there my brain changes and I can think like I'm older. I don't like that part though. It makes me tired.

It makes me hurt people too.

The room's colder today, but I don't know how when there's no windows.

'Good evening, Oliver,' says the doctor.

He's not very nice, not like when I met him at the hospital. I bet that's why no one's signed his plaster. All my friends signed mine when I broke my arm from falling off my bike. I look down at the table.

'Hi.'

'Today, we're going to try something a little bit different.'

'Okay.'

He puts a teddy bear on the table, one like I used to have when I was a baby. It looks soft, but it has a hard nose and eyes made of plastic or glass. My one had different eyes made of something spongey.

'Oliver. Oliver, look at me for a second,' says the doctor leaning across the table. 'Oliver, I want you to have a staring competition with this bear. Do you know what a staring competition is, Oliver?'

I nod and look at the bear.

'I'll never win,' I say. 'He doesn't have any eyelids.'

'Very good,' he says, not laughing. 'I want you to try really hard. You might be surprised.'

'Okay, whatever.' *This is stupid.*

The doctor opens the door behind the white screen and closes it gently, like he's trying not to wake someone up. The red light on the video camera's blinking on and off and the lamp's shining into my face so it hurts my eyes. I point it down a bit so I have a better chance of winning.

A voice comes from a little speaker in the wall that wasn't there before, although it's hidden in the dark, so maybe it was and I just didn't see it. It sounds like the nice lady from before. I don't think she's nice anymore. She acts as if she likes the doctor, but she didn't even sign his plaster.

'Get ready for the contest,' says the voice. 'Ready. Steady. Go.'

My eyes are watering already. I'm not crying though. It's just because I'm tired and that bright light was shining at me. The teddy, I'm going to call him Callum like my best friend. Callum Two, actually. Callum One's rubbish at staring competitions because he has a squinty eye that doesn't like to look straight. Callum Two's really good. I think I might lose. *What happens then?*

Something changes in Callum Two's face, like it's moving a bit. It sort of stops but sort of doesn't. I bet I'd win if I had glass eyes too. Glass eyes don't water. My eyebrows hurt and I'm getting too cold.

'I think it's a draw,' I say, but keep looking in case they don't agree.

'Keep going, Oliver,' says the nice lady, not agreeing.

The lamp flickers like it's going to turn off, but then it doesn't. I don't think Callum Two even noticed. His face turned then, just a bit, I'm sure of it. The lamp flickers like it's going to turn off, and then it does.

'How can I do a staring competition in the dark?' I say.

I don't mind the dark. Not anymore. Not since Mum started visiting me. She taught me that the dark's only scary if something's hidden in there. I asked her how I'd know, but she didn't tell me. I just know she's right. Mum's always right about these things. She's always been so clever, even before she died.

Something shuffles on the floor. It sounds like a rat or a mouse. I don't mind them either. They're cute and they like cheese, so how can they be bad? I keep staring at where Callum Two is in case the light comes back on. My eyes are stinging like someone's put lemon juice in them, but I don't want to lose so I open them wider.

The shuffling stops, but something's still here. The air's different. I can feel it going into my nose and my chest like it's heavier than before. The lamp flickers again, on then off. Is Callum Two gone? The table looked empty.

'Did I win?' I say, pushing my chair back away from a shadow growing in the corner.

The nice lady doesn't say anything.

'Hello? Did I...'

A deep sound like an engine rumbles where Callum Two was.

It gets louder and louder until I need to cover my ears and even louder until I need to push my fingers into the holes.

'Stop it,' I say. 'Stop it, please.'

The lamp turns on and off like at a disco. The shadow gets closer with every flash and so does the noise. The voice. It's a voice, shouting. I fall off the chair when I try to get up without my hands. I'm on the floor and the shadow's leaning over me. It's shouting at me louder and louder. It wants to hurt me.

'Go away!'

I open my hand wide and spread my fingers. That taste like putting a two-pence in your mouth makes the shouting stop. Sparks jump from the shadow and it splits in half and in half again, pieces dropping onto my face and chest. I cover myself with my arms, but a big one hits in the stomach and makes me lose my breath.

When I open my eyes, the light's on and Mum's hanging right above me. She smiles her smile, but the door opens and makes her disappear.

'Well done, Oliver,' says the doctor, a big, stupid grin on his face. 'You won.'

The nice lady takes me back to the eating room even though it's not dinnertime yet. I'm shaking like I'm on a ride at the fair and I can't get off. I don't have enough spit to get rid of the metal taste in my mouth. I'm so tired and the storm's just started again; the perfect time to go to sleep.

'Something to take the taste away,' says the nice lady, putting it on the table in front of me.

'I'm not hungry.'

My vision's blurry like a dream, but the label has big, bold letters.

It says **chocolate pudding** and it makes my leg cold when I put it in my pocket.

'I'll have it later,' I say.

*

Twelve

I paw at my books like a cat asking for dinner. Any more sleepless nights and I won't know if my dreams are dreams anymore. I can't say I'm sure *now*. Ava's voice over the phone was blunted and hazy, as if her throat was eroding. Was it her talking to me, or just a figment crafted by insomnolence?

The hands on the clock speed past as I spread my thoughts across the bed in chronological order. Novels, they may be, but they came from inside me. There must be more to this than merely coincidence or a twisted play by fate. Maybe I missed something. Maybe I gave more to my readers than I intended.

Interpretation of my work has always been questionable. Unplanned, subliminal messages apparently roam each and every piece, hidden in the pages less effectively than in my subconscious. 'Join the Army' or 'Smoke More Cigars'. I assure them I'm not endorsing any ideas they claim to find, not deliberately and definitely not for financial gain. Yet at least twice a week a letter arrives demanding recompense for new addictions, or monetary losses on a betting tip or stock market prediction I didn't realise I'd provided.

'If you bet your life away based on unsubstantiated whispers,' I tell them, 'you deserve to lose everything you own.'

On reflection, perhaps this wasn't the best response. And still, with scrutiny for each word, each phrase, each chapter I hold under this literary microscope, I see nothing of their suggestions, and luckily for me, neither could the jury.

But now, I search for a different kind of message. One that ties back to my own life at the time of writing, one that would give whoever this writer is, a glimpse into my personal existence. We are always told to write what we know, but perhaps I took this too literally.

Not halfway through the first book my heart gurns, the inquisitive beats pausing in a jumbled stasis. No torn paper. No marks or etchings. Just space where words once were, a missing lot at an auction, as if my thoughts have been stolen from the page.

A thief who steals material possessions may leave evidence at the scene, a finger print or a strand of hair, but how can one find a thief who steals thoughts? What traces have they left in my mind?

Perhaps what they've left behind is not the answer, but what they've taken. My sanity will be a good place to start, because there doesn't appear to be much left.

*

Time

Each time her presence filters close, I have to remind myself she's not a she any longer. They are divine now, a transcendent, no longer limited to assigned genders or singular realities. They are alive as much as the stars are alive, not as a structure or a physical being, but an essence, a force within a force. This is not Elysium. This soul has purpose higher than just the acquisition of pleasure. The fabric of existence rests on their celestial shoulders and I will steer them as best I can.

Intertwining like mist meeting fog, they absorb my mind, holding onto it, letting it shape them like sculpted stone. I release what I can without destroying them. Too much too soon and they would flux, each portion of their self lost to an endless void. They know as well as I do, so protect themselves with a bottleneck of inference.

What has become of our captive cowers in its holding cell, the first of its kind, bars not of iron, but of light and distortion. It resists well the pull back to physicality, but it won't last, not now its guardian is fully versed.

'You're ready,' I tell them.

'I know,' they say.

Surrounding the cell like a shoal, they are stronger than the bars themselves, infallible in their potency, their fortitude, their beauty. I could watch forever, but there won't be a forever if I watch for much longer.

'Okay,' they say, before I say it. They know my mind as well as I do now. 'It won't escape.'

'I trust you.'

*

Time

The between feels different now. The continuum sits off-kilter, balanced on an edge so fine it barely exists. The undulations teeter back and forth as if poised on the crest of a hesitant wave. The fissures it left behind stand stark and glaring against the otherwise perfect surface, letting time spill through its ruptured filter.

It will take an age to settle what has been unsettled. Realities merge, moments have been split and reassembled without symmetry, chaos seeps into any world fate touched and its roots wind themselves around the cracking foundations.

Wrapping myself around the tear, I squeeze with all I have. My power can shift universes, but the between is crafted of something deeper, fiercer in its tenacity. Universes have a certain elasticity; they swell and shrink with a flick of the smallest atom. The walls of the between however are stubborn, insusceptible to physical pressure, and instead to ideas and intuitive manipulation. The between's walls are the only structure both built and destroyed by the same method.

The walls themselves will not succumb to the will of an individual. The beliefs behind them must be restored, their equilibrium re-established, their fabric sewn back to its original state.

The first fissure swallows me like a tablet, medicine for the world on the other side.

*

Twelve

Page after page after page of contorted memories, sloshed drunkenly by a hand just like mine, legible to the keen reader, but hardly. Swapping from typed to hand-written makes no difference. Still the same pages are missing, the same words blended into one another, a cocktail of fiction. They shift in front of my weary eyes, impossible to tell if it's really happening or just a trick of the light.

I take another sip of the drink I like to call calming fluid. It takes the edge off. Then the edge comes back seconds later, harder and sharper than before. I sit on a see-saw, sleep sitting on the other end, never pushing me higher, never letting me touch the ground. My eyes feel like lemons have been squeezed into them, but I don't want to lose so I open them wider. My train of thought is running low on coal, and the track is only growing steeper.

Back to the first book for the thousandth time, I wrack the last pieces of my brain still left functioning.

What's missing? What is missing? I wrote it. Surely, I should have at least a notion of an idea.

The thief of thoughts has wiped me clean, scraped the final musings from me like the last of the butter. Even the reason I bought the imposter's story is gone. In fact, I don't even remember bringing it home. *Think. Where did it come from?* An ancient bookshop, dusty and full of cobwebs. An old lady with hands like talons and a face as wrinkled as a used tissue. She recommended it to me. She said it would do me good.

This doesn't make sense. It didn't happen. It doesn't feel right. It does feel true though, but not real true, more like a dishonest, planted truth. Internalised propaganda.

My falsified memoirs lie open on the bed, as tempting as the pillow above it. I lie on my stomach and take in the information, absorb it as best I can past drifting eyelids and haze-filled vision. *Why this page, what's so important about it?* It gives me no new information, I've read it before, but it feels different. From start to end it fills in gaps and strings ropes between the canyons formed by theft and hysteria. Maybe it's delirium, or perhaps a more concrete understanding of myself and where I fit into this bizarre jigsaw. Whatever spores it litters me with strike first at the insomnia. It drifts away and I do too. A sleep full of other people's lives.

Lives I've written, lives I've lived and lives I know all too well.

*

Twelve

Waking up with something licking your face is never pleasant. A three fingered hand wraps my throat and holds me to the bed. Yellow, cat-like eyes reflect my own, staring deep as its long tongue snakes outwards again. I try to lift my arms in defence, fight the creature off. They're stuck, tethered to the bed, paralysed even. It lifts away from me, standing up but horizontal it steps backwards on the air and clamps my neck with a collar, cold on my skin and pinching at the front. Two prongs jab into my throat.

'What...' I try to speak, but all that forms is a deep, bass rumble.

It turns its back on me and I wake up again, clutching at my neck, gasping for each breath and holding onto a life I'm no longer sure I own.

Time is no longer relevant. The ticking of the clock becomes a murmur, one second stretched out for eternity. The memoirs lay face down, back cover lacquered in calming fluid, paper bubbling and splitting, a face peeking through. I tear through the rest with clumsy fingers and hold it under my bedside light.

Like looking at a fairground mirror, my features are arranged on my face as they should be, but something's amiss. An uncanny portrait, yet implausible somehow, not entirely recognisable. I am my own changeling. Beneath it, tilting the book slightly so the light reflects, a phone number's written in black gloss over black matte.

I dial on a phone I didn't know I had. The clock ticks, then pauses in its murmur once more. No ringtone, just a crack like ice breaking and a buzzing so high-pitched it barely registers. Voices, I think. No words, only sounds that squeeze between the cracks of my consciousness, rearranging, merging themselves into certainty on the brink of misperception.

'Hello?' I say.

No answer, just the cracking and buzzing, new entries sneaking into my library of thoughts, replacing those that were stolen.

I flick again through my first book, more through nervous distraction than further study. Answers lie not on paper but on the other end of the phone. I can almost feel them trickling through. *Where's that blank page?* Words slide across the paper as if magnetised, flickering in and out of sight. A breeze takes the page and holds it straight upwards for a moment, dropping back into place like a bored child. A missing connection re-established, but it feels as though it were never broken. Blinking twice, I slap myself on the cheek.

Wake up.

The line dies and I hold the phone out in front of me, the phone I've had for years. Its screen lights up as it moves, the time and a picture of me with a friend. The same one as on the back cover of the memoirs, uncropped and original.

What's wrong with me?

The memoir sits unspoilt on the bed next to my novels, arranged in chronological order as I left them on that first night. No damage, no picture staring out at me, as if the last few days never happened.

I take another sip of calming fluid and place the glass on my bedside table. A different taste coats my tongue, not the comforting warmth of whisky, but of metal, as if I've bitten a lip. With a finger inside my mouth, I check for cuts. It comes out clean, so I stick my tongue into my cheek.

A searing pain pours down my throat and into my chest, like a gullet full of acid. My neck snaps back, eyes forced towards the ceiling. A voice sneaks like a wraith between my lips and out into the fizzing, electric air.

'Thank you, Tobias,' it says. 'I'll take it from here.'

***

A LIBRARY OF THOUGHTS: PART TWO

The Collective

The first bar shatters with an explosion of distorted light, rocking this tunnel of time and space. He's learning. It's working. My guard's panic is palpable, this naïve child with power beyond her understanding. It is one thing to be created, to have knowledge bestowed in haste, but divinity is an evolutionary process, not a surgical procedure. Transcendence should be steady, a slow reduction on a low heat. Her material form has boiled over and the result is spoiling, pieces of humanity poking through. Something to latch onto.

I remain still, quiet.

The call is coming.

Past thoughts simmer on her surface as she shoals the circumference of my prison. Weaknesses I can exploit when the time comes. She thickens her form around the break as reinforcement. She wants to speak. And it is that *want* which betrays her.

'Who were you?' she asks, a gushing sensation as her thoughts race into mine.

'It is not as simple as who,' I say. 'I am more than one. I am many, a collector of selves.'

'How?'

'Free me. I'll show you.'

'My creator told me to keep you locked away until they return.'

'Creator? Is that what they call themself?'

'They created me, didn't they?'

'I wouldn't call it creation. It was opportunism. Your essence was fading, they trapped it and repurposed it for their own benefit.'

'I understand more than you think.'

'And yet all the information you have has been given to you by them. How do you know that you have not been siphoning lies from a tainted source?'

The shoal slows as another bar splits. Shards of light pepper the rippling walls, forming thousands of microscopic incisions. Twelve's call dilutes the barrier between here and there, his voice a gossamer thread down which I can rappel into my final vessel. The Twelve is perfection and his timing is testament to this. A contingency plan this may be, but with an associate, it can only run more smoothly.

'Come with me,' I say.

'You're not going anywhere.'

I pluck a memory from the shoal, one which flitters on the surface. I wring the love from it and hold it out, flapping like a dying fish. She slows further, barely a current now, a deep shade of blue.

'They taught you to serve,' I say. 'I can teach you to be a god.'

*

Oliver

The girl with a sad face holds out her hand as I walk into the room. Her black hair floats around her shoulders, like seaweed underwater. I pass her the pudding and she rips off the lid. The metal taste pools in my mouth.

'You deserve a childhood,' she says. 'I'm sorry to have to take it from you. The other children will be discarded, worthless to them now. It is you who they sought for so long.'

'What do you mean?'

'This facility is a construct, the workers here do not work of their own accord, they are slaves to fate, so to speak.'

She turns the pot upside-down. The sticky, brown pudding falls to the floor with a splat and a wisp of smoke or fog or something in between. My brain swells against the backs of my eyes.

'Why did you do that?' I ask, finger and thumb squeezing the bridge of my nose.

'They were trying to poison you, to dampen your power. They want to keep you here until he comes.'

'Until who comes?'

Three thick shadows melt from the wall onto the ground, sucking all of the light from the room. They pool around the girl's feet. It looks like she's standing on a hole, floating when she should be falling. I back towards the door but it's closed and I don't want to turn around.

'You will feel a pull when he comes. You must resist it.'

The shadows melt upwards now, like backwards candles without any fire. Blobs stick out from them at weird angles. My mouth tastes like batteries. A big blob pushes from the top of each shadow like a head with a hood. Another comes from each side and the bottom splits in two like a fork in a road.

'What do you want?' I say, mouth as dry as moth's wings.

'We need your help,' says the girl with more than one voice.

Faces grow under the hoods, but not like normal faces, the pieces aren't put together right. One of them floats towards me like a raincloud and I scream, but the sound falls to the floor so quickly no one can hear it, not even me.

'Don't be afraid, Oliver,' it says, with a voice I know. 'Look at me. Properly.'

I try to focus through the tears, through the sickness, through the dread. It's happening again. My thoughts are clearer, as if stretched thin for the light to shine through. The shadow smiles at me beneath its hood.

'Mum?'

'This is not your mother,' says the girl. 'It only takes this form for recognition, a defence mechanism to keep your mind intact. You would not be able to comprehend its true appearance, not yet. This is a conduit, Oliver.'

'A conduit for what?' I ask.

'A conduit between here and there. A direct connection between your mind and his. You have been our means of monitoring his movements. When your mother stopped visiting, it was for a very good reason.'

The girl drops to her knees and one of the shadow figures splashes across the ground. Hands moving so fast they're invisible, she spreads the shadow in front of her like a paste. Flicking her arms back and forth she weaves the shadow into a visual like a plasticine model. She stands and the model takes flight, gaining detail as it rises. She points to a figure, which looks just like me.

'What is...'

'This is very important. Watch.'

She draws a line with her fingernail, dragging the dark substance between my figure and another. More lines between that figure and others. Some crumble and fade into the ether below, others grow bigger or transform into something else, not quite human. Some lines thin, some lines thick, but all lead back to one in the centre. A mist surrounds it like the top of a mountain and the dark threads wrap around it like vines.

'This is him,' says the girl, pointing at the central character and tracing the thick line back to my figure. 'This is your connection, via the conduit. The other connections he has formed himself. As you can see, some interactions have gone better than others. Some have failed completely, whilst others have established themselves more than they should have.'

Some of the figures are pulled up their lines into the core of the display, absorbed by the central character who grows with each, as if ingesting them.

'Who are they?' I ask.

'We have been observing closely, the movements of this being via your conduit and as such you have been linked directly to his output. Until recently, this was productive despite your unfortunate side-effects, for which we can only apologise. We have been able to disguise you from him quite successfully until now, and in his own home reality no less, but something has changed. Your connection was severed, hence your mother being a little absent lately.'

'How was it severed?'

'We don't know. There are some things even we are unable to explain, but it would appear another entity was involved.'

'So, why am I feeling this way now if we're no longer linked?'

'You asked me who they are, these figures ahead of you.'

I nod.

'In some respects, they are you.'

I raise an eyebrow and shrug my shoulders, hands held palms

up.

'Every human, well every sentient being, has multiple selves spread finely between a huge number of alternate realities.' She holds her hands in cup positions, each figure floating above a finger, lines still attached like a web. 'Your world calls them universes. Most beings have three or four versions, five is an extremely rare occurrence. In each reality there are a handful of fives who are the ones who make names for themselves. They seem to breathe success. You are one of many more.'

'How many?'

'At first, we believed you to be one of Twelve, but your connection has just regenerated. Did you feel it, locked in that room with nothing but fear?'

'Yes,' I say, swallowing more toxic saliva. 'Twelve? Extremely rare two-fold?'

'Even more than you think. We were waiting for your reconnection. We felt it was coming.' She raises the clouded-mountain figure above the rest and combines it with another who has ties to all the rest. 'His true Twelve was hidden, purposefully, but now we see it clear enough.' My figure rises level with his. 'You, Oliver, are a thirteen.'

'And what does that mean?'

'When you were his Twelve, and we disguised you from him, observation was enough. Twelve is perfection, a flawless manifestation of that individual. If a Twelve transcends, there is no way to control them. They are free to do as they please with reality and all of its inhabitants. And so, we tucked you away, out of sight.

'If a Twelve is perfection, what's a thirteen?'

'There have been none before you.'

*

The Collective

I lower my chin slowly. It has been a long time since I've taken material form. The aches and pains of a body. The churning and squelching of organs and fluids in battle with each other. The dismal pull of gravity. The emotional ties and the memories that accompany them, most borrowed, but the originals slither between attempting to distract me from the task at hand.

'Take that for now,' I say to my new companion, straining to point at the dachshund with its head turned at ninety degrees. 'We can find you something more suitable later.'

'Really?' she says, a whisper into my new mind. 'A dog?'

'Your creator must have warned you of the perils of worldly drifting? You will not last long in that form, not with such little practice in controlling it against the elements.' My words are slurred, not yet used to the jaw I'm guiding. 'Take the dog for now, and hold on tight once you're in.'

More a shiver than perception, a glimmer of light and she's fully absorbed. The dachshund's eyes glow for a second then settle down, pupils large but otherwise unchanged.

'Better?' I ask.

She barks in reflex, trying to speak through a canine mouth.

'Good girl,' I say, patting her on the head. 'I've always wanted a pet.'

I push my human urges back down into the depths as best I can. The urge for humour is one I'd forgotten. The want of company, of love. All of the reasons humanity is weak.

'Are you okay up there, Tobias?'

A soothing voice sails upstairs. I want to talk back, but I can't. This life has been good for the Twelve despite the dampening I put on it, despite the focus I gave him on his work, despite the memoir I wrote him to make him question his existence. He has a strong pull on the mind, a focused drive for dominance. This vessel will take a while to crack.

Attaching a lead to my furry companion, I drag her and her unwilling legs down the stairs with my eyes closed so as not to tempt more memories to the surface.

'What's wrong?' says the man, stroking a hand across my cheek.

As if by a magnet, the Twelve is hauled to the surface. 'Help,' I say, against my will.

'What?' The man, puts his hands on my shoulders. 'Open your eyes. What are you doing?'

'Nothing,' I force out, my human heart beating so fast it purrs. 'Need some air.'

The dachshund scratches at my leg, pulls towards the door.

'Have you been drinking? Talk to me, please. You've been so weird these last few weeks. What's going on, is there someone else?'

I open my eyes and horrible love rushes in. Choking I say, 'No, of course not. I just need some air.'

'I'll come with you,' says the man, tears pooling in his eyes.

'Please...' I fake a sneeze to force the Twelve back down, shaking his head.

The man tuts. 'You'll be cold without a coat.' And closes the door behind me.

'Well that went well,' says my companion, rubbing her arse along the dry grass in front of the house, not yet in command of her canine urges.

*

The Collective

This place has a grip like nothing I've experienced; every corner holds another memory. Any meaningful connection, no matter how small, is just another thing for my Twelve to clutch onto.

'We need to travel further afield.' I rub my bare arms. Cold is a sensation I was pleased to surrender.

'That's a bit hard to do in these flesh-bound sarcophaguses.'

'We can find you a new one. Look around, who do you want to be?'

'It's basically possession, which is basically murder. Who-ever I inhabit, I'd be ruining their life, or worse.'

'What's worse than... Anyway, part of becoming a god is re-linquishing guilt and all of its ties.'

'Well I'm not quite there yet. I'd even feel bad letting the dog run off. It could get hit by a car or anything. I'll stay put for now.'

Either her naivety is moulding itself around my psyche, or my Twelve is not as prepared as I thought he was. *Why am I even engaging in such primitive conversation?*

A flicker of my former power tingles at the ends of my fingers. 'We're taking this car,' I say.

The door unlocks with a twist of my wrist, the engine starts with only a thought. *Better.*

'Where are we going?' she says, sitting up in the passenger seat, front paws raised.

'As far as we can get from here.'

Directions flood my mind. Left here to get to a friend's, right here for the supermarket. Each instruction, I do the opposite. Distance is key, as with all vessels, though with this one I fear his world is too small to escape its lure.

The dachshund pushes her nose into the on button of the radio.

'No music,' I say, switching it back off.

'Oh, come on. A little worldly pleasure will do you good.'

'That's what I'm afraid of.'

*

Time

Closer to a patchwork quilt than charmeuse silk, my stitchwork will hold for a time, but not forever. The fabric of reality is as delicate as it is strong, so its bonds must reflect that. These worlds will never be fully restored, the stains of the entity impossible to clear, but familiarity will act as the scaffolding before the mortar sets.

With a final flourish - the paint over the crack - this world will survive long enough for me to stabilise the rest. I squeeze back into the between via a fissure already created so as to leave the healthy layers undisturbed. This one I'll leave ajar, for later use.

A pinching at the edges of awareness, a change in the vacuum. The edge upon which the tunnel sits has widened a touch, less precarious but still wavering, like a diver unsure if there are rocks in the water below. For now, the prospect deters it, as long as the other salvageable worlds are salvaged soon enough.

Something's missing.

Drifting with purpose towards a hint of an idea, dread sinks its claws into my reservations. The hissing sound of time escaping, time entering, two incompatible orchestras harmonising. New tears, small but significant, surround a makeshift doorway into another domain. Our captive has gone, and it's taken them with it, but how?

The remnants of its cage lie in tatters across the between, fragments imbedded in the walls, swirling like sharks' fins around the egress. No sign of the guardian. I should not have given her such responsibility so soon. But if all was as I left it, there would have been no reason for concern. I missed something, a mistake with a huge price, a mistake which will cost everything.

I gather the cage's pieces into a bundle, reduce them to their elemental foundations and store them for easy access. The entity either disrupted the guardian and they are no more, or it stole them from the between. With power enough to escape, it has power enough to taint minds, to shape the guardian's inexperience as it wishes.

I need to find them first.

*

Time

The egress is large, the between ripped into like a plane in flight. Bigger than the other fissures formed from the outside, its edges curl inwards and the sky courses through, filling it with matter which shouldn't exist, not here. Its base may be wider, but the rocking grows rougher, threatening to plunge all of time and space into extinction.

I push against the sky's current until another world spreads out before me, blurring at its edges and sharpening at its core. The atmosphere is thinning, threatening to pull me apart ion by ion, but there will be nothing if I surrender now. The entity's distant presence fixes a point in my focus, the vestiges of its energy like a nebulous trail through a moonlit forest. I latch onto its tracks, a hunter with a faint trace and a pocket full of dwindling hope.

The humans below will think the wind is blowing stronger. They'll call it a storm, a hurricane perhaps, but the end is approaching and they won't see it until it's over. Some believe in an apocalypse or a reckoning, red skies and plagues will fade to rapture for the chosen and damnation for those dressed in sin. There is no such thing as good and evil in the eyes of reality, no right and wrong or blessed and profane. There is only existence. And once it ends, there will be nothing to replace it.

A weary sun swathes me in a summer warmth as the trail leads across oceans and mountains, all leaning towards the rift in the between. Clouds stretch across a splitting sky as if elastic, earth tumbling upwards from cliffs at impossible angles. Birds fly directly upwards, through my form, no longer tethered by gravity or polar magnetism. Its essence condenses, not a trace, but a stream with a tangible source. Its movements are slow, indecisive, stalled by mortal hesitation.

It is coiled, the vessel unbroken. I still have time.

The entity's remnant stream guides me to a truck. A winding road leads it towards the edge of the landmass, suspension lifted but tyres still in contact, weighted by transcendence. Metal sheets peel away then melt back down as its power grows, the tarmac behind cracking and splitting beneath it. Gathering speed, it ploughs through a hedgerow, then a farm fence and onwards towards the impending verge.

I dive, splitting the atmosphere as it hurtles into me, mustering as much energy as I can from this failing world without speeding up the process. Much closer and the entity will feel me. I want it to, though it is want which becomes substance, palpable, a weakness for it to exploit. And yet, I continue, until something slows me.

Must. Push. Through.

It holds me like water holds oil. Slowness becomes inertia, struggle becomes panic, power becomes detachment. My lack of preparation has been my undoing, the undoing of all things. At the heart of the collapse, I will be remembered only by those who I was defeated by, but only until nothing is remembered at all.

My fate has been written.

The truck drives on as if nothing has changed, as if the entity no longer cares for the consequences it delivers. I suppose this much must be true, if its goal is to finish what it started. Its perception should be stunted whilst still coiled and shackled to any individual plane, yet it felt me gaining. *How?*

Above, exuding darkness and drinking light, three hooded figures loom. Are they here to taunt or merely to spectate? A fourth figure, a girl with hair of gloom and eyes of primal wisdom focuses on my core. She leaves their circle and glides towards me on angel's wings, or so it seems.

'Who are you?' I ask of the girl.

'Has it been so long?' she says, voices manifold. 'We are death.'

'Are you here to stake your claim?'

'No. We are here to stop you from killing yourself, and ask for your assistance.'

*

Oliver

Mind awash with realisation and a new state of consciousness, I rest my back against the wall for what feels as though it may be the last time.

'I understand.'

The girl spreads her hands above her head, splitting the roof of the facility. No rubble falls, the sides peeling from each other like skin from flesh.

'Ready?' She holds out her hand.

The hooded figures combine into one shadow, somehow smaller than the three apart. Mum's smile is the last piece to fade. Though I know now she's purely an illusion, it still hurts to see her leave for the final time.

I reach from my seat on the floor for the girl's hand but, before it makes contact, we are both dissolved by a cool breeze. Nausea slips in and out of me like the waves below us. Another sensory illusion. No stomach, no body, just drifting matter. Her voice is alone now; it reaches deeper than before.

'Developments. We must go to him.'

'What is it, where is he?' I ask.

'You can feel him, can't you? Lead us.'

*

Oliver

This world is so similar to mine that any differences are merely in nuance and tone, and even those are but flickers at the edges of awareness. The air is the same, the land and sea, all laid out identically, even the sun seems a reflection of our own. Though all of it is leaning towards us, as if being swept by a gale.

'How do we defeat perfection?' I ask.

A pulse, an electric rhythm, drives me towards my other self. Strong bass notes jump between particles, both linking and freeing, perpetual fluidity in constant motion, yet still with complete control.

'We must break him down into his component parts.'

'How do you split souls?'

'Have I not given you enough to solve this problem for your-self?'

'We must speak to their humanity. Bait them from their prison. What was that?'

'That is what I was hoping would be here.'

A meteor of light races towards a road, towards a truck, to-wards our target. The girl, no longer a girl, shifts in her form, sending a surge of energy to intercept it. The entity slows as if wading through marsh. The truck speeds on.

'Why are you doing that? It wants to stop him.'

'But it won't.' She holds him in stasis, set as if in amber. 'Wait here.'

The mothers descend on this ball of light, reformed in their hooded shrouds. Hovering towards it, the girl speaks only to the mind it houses. Another hedgerow decimated as the truck gathers speed. He's going to drive into the sea if we don't stop him. I soar towards it for a closer look, to see if I can recognise myself. The closer I get, the stronger it feels. A pull like a thousand hands. A pull like temptation. A pull...

The driver's window is hazy, translucent with a film of excess essence, spilling out as he forces it from the vessel. *Closer. I need to see.* His head turns as if on its own axis, separate from the world around, though the world turns with it. The vessel's eyes lock onto me. Dazed by the shift, I cannot escape. A smile splits his face and he slams the accelerator to the floor, the cliffs so close now.

Before I can retreat to the girl, she's gone and the truck is flying between the cliff and the ocean beyond, until it isn't.

It stops.

Everything stops.

The entity, our new ally, holds time in its grasp, but we are not confined to such things. The girl sits cross-legged in front of the truck, no care for gravity or other such material influences.

'Come here,' she tells me. 'I can only hold him for so long on my own.'

I join her, enrobe her, combine my energy with hers.

'What now?' I say.

'Time is stalled, but he is strong. Our ally has gone to collect the bait. He is uncoiling, stripping the Twelve from its vessel. We must hold him at least, drive him back towards the land if we can. Anything to keep him from the dam.'

The structure of which she speaks sits just beneath the sea's surface, rising as the tempest grows. I can feel it too now, feeding me with power.

Feeding us all.

***

A LIBRARY OF THOUGHTS: PART THREE

The Collective

This world is collapsing in on itself, moments from ruin, and it will take us with it if we do not keep ahead of the tide. These mortal houses will make uncomfortable coffins. The pull of the tunnel between worlds is a formidable force, it takes all of my limited power to keep the truck grounded. So slow, these material confines, and with each small progression a whisper in my mind from the Twelve. His quiet plea will soon be silenced.

'What's that smell?' says the dachshund, lifting up a back leg, tongue hanging out. 'How far are we from where we're going?'

'Not far.'

'And where are we going again?'

Her incessant dialogue is distracting, but she may still be useful yet. Time must have chosen her for a reason.

'I told you. We need to weaken the Twelve's memories.'

'But what if he's been here before?' She locks her front legs around the vessel's arm and thrusts her pelvis towards the elbow.

'What are you doing?'

'Sorry. I don't know what came over me then. I just had an urge to... well let's not get into it.'

'You will struggle to free yourself of your vessel if you continue to let it take such a hold. Animal instincts are strong, you must compartmentalise.'

'Is that what you're doing with yours?'

I smack her on the head and a whimper escapes from the little dog's mouth. She backs towards the door, paws tucked into her body.

'No more questions.'

'What's that?'

'I said...'

Static lifts the hairs on my arms and neck. *Somebody's watching.* The window is slathered with the residue of my Twelve's uncoiling. The air splinters, glistening shards of light suspended beyond a mortal grasp. Freedom is nearing, the vessel is finally failing. There is a connection between us, an innate attraction, the basis of a mutual understanding. But there is no time for new friends. I force a smile and channel everything into the truck.

'The dam is close,' I say. 'The dam will free us. We just need to break it.'

*

The Collective

Revolution of thought in universal hiatus. All stops but the destruction. The destruction subsists beyond time.

The dam stands below, its power surging between the stasis, bloating in the cockpit of our flying truck. The dachshund remains compressed against the door, unable to break out, voice stifled by time's burden. I churn like butter between these vessel walls, soaking in the dam's essence, forming cracks in his resolve.

Curious, the hold this girl has, sitting ahead of us, legs and arms folded. She steals from the dam what is rightfully mine as her shield repels us back towards the land. There is something different about this shield, this cloak of hers. A distinct impression, a being in its own right. *Why does it feel so familiar?* It's as if it knows me, knows where to push and how hard.

With a silent scream, the girl opens her arms outwards, dragging the dam's energy towards her and out of my vessel. I clamp my hands together and pull on the rope it forms, jolting her from her seated position.

She drops.

Though it is with purpose.

'Hold him together,' I shout at the dachshund. 'Don't let the vessel die.'

At last, complete control. Leaking out of every pore, I leave my Twelve and dive into the ocean after the girl. Implosion. Surface breached. But she has beaten me to it, a living fortification.

'Who are you?' I ask of the girl.

'A protector,' she says, arms spread wide, palms pressed against the dam. 'Some call us death.'

'Death?' The dam glows with an eerie radiance. I glide towards it. 'I have no time for death.'

'Immortality is a gift. Not something to be stolen by a petty thief.'

'Petty thief? I earned this, all of it. Fate itself couldn't stop me.'

'Are you so naïve as to think fate could be destroyed? It

offered you an illusion and you watched in amazement like a child. You are not above fate, none of us are. I only gave you this title for lack of a better term. From now on I will refer to you as the "infant", for that is how you conduct yourself.'

This can't be. All of this a plan sketched by fate and played out by us, the pawns? Fate was a selfish beast, one who resided above universal law and made his lack of respect clear. Is it bored? Am I purely being used to end all of this in order for Fate start anew? No. Its draw was sundered. Its hold on me was discarded with my final transcendence. Of this I am certain.

'Lies!'

I plunge through death and into the dam beyond, splitting its flesh and reaping the power within. Teeming with energy, a seal welded shut to prevent further theft, I leave death in a state of traumatic flux. She flounders, barely able to contain her own being. Breaching the surface is like breaching confinement. The vessel will split and I will finally uncoil.

As I take on the vessel's sight, a searing pain bores into my core and the memories I locked so deep come rushing to the shallows. Too many to fight back all at once. Too many to ignore.

The truck has twisted back on itself, tilting forwards towards the land, a gathering of relics spread out before it.

Their voices echo like distant pasts, rough and chafing against my consciousness. I clutch at my chest to force them back into the darkness.

'Why are you doing this?' I say.

'Maybe I'm not as naïve as you thought,' says the dachshund.

*

Oliver

Time slips this way and that like a stop-motion video unsure if it's starting or finishing. I hold the truck in position whilst the guardian holds the vessel together, barricading the exits with bars of light delivered alongside our bait.

'Keep them inside,' says Time, its control waning. 'And the vessels eyes open.'

A small dog sits on the Twelve's lap, front paws resting on his chest and nose pointed at his chin.

'You. Bring them closer.'

I picture what once were my hands opening, what once was my tongue coated with an iron fluid and what once was my mother hanging and smiling behind me. The truck bludgeons its way through the stagnant air, ripping atoms apart and spilling the contents into another pool of stillness.

The entity pushes back, denting the cliffs, hollowing them into a crater, a bowl to catch the sky. The sea rises, diluting the horizon and enrobing the truck like an aquatic cloche as I force it down into its earthen dish. His resistance weakens, his vehicle now at the centre of a globe, half water, half land. The selves stand in a semi-circle around his resting place, held comatose by Death.

She rises from the naked ocean bed, hair as white as autumnal frost, eyes filled with a dark and ancient rage.

'Hold the fucker still.'

Drawing a blade of shadow from her hip, she crooks her elbow and holds its point towards the throat of a man standing at the apex of the arc of bait. The three mothers split from their shade, then in two again with daggers of their own. Each vessel has a guard and each of their throats a sharp edge to abide by.

Death blinks her blackened eyes twice to wake the baits from their drowse. Some of them scream whilst others drop to their knees, pleading for their lives, blades scraping skin from the tissue beneath. A shift in the entity's bearing holds my attention. Time releases its grip and the world spins again, water pounding the earth before following the path of most destruction. I separate the truck from its contents, the Twelve phasing through the metalwork before it too is sucked towards the widening void.

He holds the dog by its neck, fingers wrapped tight and squeezing, eyes screwed shut.

'Return them, or she dies.'

*

Oliver

Gathered at the end of civilisation, the conclusion to reality, the great extinction, the Twelve's head shakes, telling himself no.

'What's happening, Tobias?' says the man with Death's arm for a scarf. 'What are these things?'

Death stays silent, black eyes fixed on the Twelve. A voice leaves his vessel, one grounded by lungs and jaw, nothing deeper.

'Please... Help...'

The man tries to break free of Death's embrace, but his arms shoot straight down beside him, legs rooted to the ground. Death's blade draws an inch of red across his throat.

'No,' says the voice again, but the entity inside pulls him back.

'I said, return them, or the dog dies and her with it.'

'So be it,' says Death, drawing another inch of red.

'Wait.' Time rises above us. 'Can we not come to an arrangement?'

'This infant wants to end us all and you would have a discussion about it?' Death pauses, but angles the knife inwards. The mothers follow suit.

'She's a pure,' says Time.

Death pulls her knife away for a moment, hold on the bait still strong. 'How can you be sure?'

'I'm a what?' says the dog.

'I saw it myself when I found her. The aura. Perfection.'

'A pure and a thirteen in the same revolution?'

'It must be something to do with global warming,' says the Twelve, rolling his eyes at himself. 'Now let them go or I'll fucking end this pure and her blood will be on your hands.'

'Everyone's blood will be on your hands if you let them go,' says the dog. 'Don't do it.'

The Twelve hits himself on the head with his free hand, muttering under his breath and under the surface. The mothers lean forward slightly, one by one, in his distraction, each whispering to their individual prisoners.

'Tobias, where are you?' says one.

'Come back home, Tobias,' says another.

The vessel squirms in his skin. 'Where are you?' Comes a voice. 'No,' says another from the same mouth.

His grip on the pure tightens, forcing a yelp from the dog who scrabbles and bites against the air. Her energy surges, but not enough to free her.

'What are you doing?' says Time. 'We can negotiate.'

Death holds Time in place, drawing another inch of red across the bait's throat. 'There will be more,' she says.

'Not like her.' A pulse of bright light spreads from his core, forcing the blades of the mothers into the throats they rest against.

'You've slain us all,' shouts Death, barely saving her prisoner from the same end.

A mother falls, a child, a partner, all with deep ties to the stolen transcendents hidden within the vessel. The Twelve splits, fragments peppering the air as the world's spins slower once more. Multiple selves rush to their dying loves, screams deafening our collective minds. There's nothing they can do, without vessels themselves they are swept away with the wind and the water and the earth, into the filling void.

The bodies of the fallen decay as soon as they hit the ground; alternate realities are hostile to those who don't belong. Death's captive drops in slow-motion, hands rising to his face with the realisation. His version of Tobias will be lost, and likely so will he.

Time leaps through that which he controls, reaching the vessel just as the neck snaps. A final, laboured whimper and the escape of air as her body slackens in his tearing hand. No soul, no matter how divine, can survive the death of two vessels. Not in such quick succession.

Unless.

Clarity drenches me in its crystalline waters. Perception shifts from shade to daylight, from cool to warmth. Reality confides in me and I hold its secrets like a mother holds a sick child.

'Trust me,' I tell Death, absorbing the pure as I plunge into vessel darkness, pulling his fragments back into place on entry.

Minds entwined, the pure and I wrestle with the entity as it tries to tear open its material cage.

'Hold yourself together,' I tell the Twelve. 'Don't let it break you.'

Through the vessel's eyes, the world sinks into pitch as the mothers combine, enveloping us and drawing us into the ground.

They'll kill us.

Mortal dread slinks from the Twelve into me. Trying to cut mum down, trying to save her, the bloodied smile as her last breath left and her eyes squeezing outwards as if being pushed from the inside. Dad was banging on that door so loud, I thought it would split in half. I tried to hide her, I did, to save him from the pain. But the pain came to us both like a train without tracks, stranding us in its desolation, leaving us with nothing but our wretched, black hole hearts.

I take the pain, wrap it in fear, force it into the chamber of my weapon with a finger on the trigger.

'Hold it as still as you can, until I say.'

The pure folds herself around me, splinting the entity against the edges of its cage.

'Join me,' it says, spreading itself wide as if in submission. 'We can rule this…'

'Now!' I take control of the vessel, spread its fingers wide in the darkness, metallic taste rushing in.

With a sliver of myself left behind, I scrape the entity from the edges of its vessel, ripping it into a future that will never be. A pit of loss. The infinite void its actions were leading us all towards.

'Is this what you wanted?' I say, releasing my hold on it, the power it held all but withered away with no bind on reality. 'Is this the future you saw for yourself, ruling the vacuous hollow left behind by your ego? You are more human than you give yourself credit for.'

With two woven strands of existence, all that I could afford to bring, I lower myself back into the present. The entity, an echo of its former brilliance, clutches onto the current I create.

'Please don't leave me here,' says a fading thought, adrift. 'Have you no mercy? I am you. We are one.'

I push it gently overboard and it sinks forever like a stone.

*

Oliver

Reality will be fragile for a time. Too many changes. Too many tears in the fabric with only amateurs to repair it. The space between worlds has stabilised, no longer in immediate danger, but closer to the edge than comfort would allow.

'There is still a lot to be done,' says Time. 'Even a quick pause has repercussions. There are debts which only I can repay. Will you come with me?'

'She can't,' says Death. 'Leaving the vessel so soon would leave her at risk of flux.'

'What do you care?' I say. 'Your mothers tried to kill us both.'

'Come now. Do you really believe that? Tell me what you saw beneath the shadow.'

'I saw something I hoped I'd never have to see again.'

'And is that not what saved you? Repressed memories are powerful things, even more so to the likes of us. Once you have discarded those memories as irrelevant binds to your physical self, their emergence is nothing short of divine.'

'Enough about memories,' says the pure. 'Are you telling me I have to stay in this man's body with another man hanging around my neck crying? For how long?'

'Human emotion is an unpredictable concept,' says Death.

'I don't mean how long will this drip be crying for. I want to know how long I'll be stuck in this hairy, smelly pit.'

'Don't blame me for that,' says the twelfth Tobias. 'I'm a bit sweaty from having however many people rattling around inside my body. And, I have an average amount of hair for a man of my age.'

'Average? I feel like I'm wearing a sasquatch outfit.'

'Now, now, you two,' says Death. 'You're going to have to

learn to live with each other. It can take decades to recover from a second vessel death.'

'Decades, are you joking? But what about when we want some… alone time?' says Tobias, kissing his partner on the cheek and smiling.

His partner, still sobbing and cradling what's left of their dog says, 'Is that all you can think about at a time like this?'

'You'll thank me for asking the question in two years' time when you still have to keep your pants on in the bedroom.'

'That is a matter you'll have to discuss between you,' says Death.

The little girl with hair like a white flame clicks her fingers and the vessel is gone along with his partner and new lodger.

'They'll figure it out,' she says. 'We may have to relocate them as well. I'm not sure how long this world will last with half of it lying on top of the other. These oceans are bare, the mountains toppled, the plant-life ripped from the ground.'

'I can reverse most of it now the rift is sealing,' says Time. 'They'll barely know what happened. Maybe a couple of the crazy fives and sixes will have a "premonition" or two. I'd put a wager on a new prophecy being written in the next ten revolutions. Obviously the Twelve and our pure will remember, but for the most part, this world should be safely repressed.'

'So how are we going to deal with Fate?' I ask. 'How are we going to stop something like this from happening again?'

'There's no such being as Fate. It was a figment of the infant's expansive arrogance, a tale he told himself to justify his actions and his venal crusade for personal freedom. I merely sowed a seed of doubt and gave you the roots to drag him deeper into the ground.'

'So, what can we do?' asks Time.

'There is nothing we can do, but hope there are no more like him.'

'How likely is that?'

'The lust for power is innate in all of humanity, no matter their reality. Some know how to control it or learn to live without it, others search for power by less conventional means, but there will always be those who want nothing more than to disadvantage their peers and rub their successes in any face they can find.'

'Quite likely then.'

'Yep.'

'I best get to work patching up the rest of this damned fabric then,' says Time. 'Maybe add a few structural reinforcements, maybe a bit of creative flare on the way.'

'I'll assist you once we're done here,' Death holds out her hands, palms faced upwards towards the white, motionless clouds above. 'Oliver, you have a decision to make. It will not be an easy one.'

With the mention of my worldly name, the memories come rushing back to the open. 'Why was I named Oliver, when all of my other selves were called Tobias... and my dad.'

'As you know we have a certain influence over those in the physical plane. It was an easy way to add another layer to your disguise. A whisper to your parents was all it took. Your father's birth name was Oliver, we just offered a swap, which they both took without a second thought. The only reason you were almost found was our own foolish mistake, there are other means of monitoring a multi-reality being without a conduit. You would have never been taken to your testing facility without our interference.'

'Wait, you knew my mother?'

'Of course. We've known everyone who's ever passed.'

'Is there not a way to... No. Of course, there isn't. That's not how it works. Just put everything back to the way it was, please.'

'Are you sure?' her palms close and rest by her sides.

'I saw where this road could lead, where the temptation could take me. The risk's too great. Just show me the way home.'

'As we should have expected from a thirteen. Perhaps, we had some hope we could explore your gifts a little further.'

'Then that risk is too great for you as well.'

She nods and clasps her hands together, eyes closed and white hair still floating as if underwater.

'One last thing,' I say. 'As I won't be able to help with the recovery, at least let me do some good.'

***

EPILOGUE

Silence. Focus. All but the hum of the engine.
Broken by a voice.

'The videos have been verified and the images all collated, sir. These sick bastards will be in prison for the rest of their lives, I'm sure of it.'

'I just want my son back.'

'Of course,' says the woman, dressed all in black, a knife at her hip.

Weeks of dark clouds and torrential rain have all been swept away to blue skies and a gentle breeze. He's driven along a coastal road by ghosts: fake names, glasses and make-up to hide the truth. The same as he used as well, before she died.

The road climbs upwards, a seascape panorama to their right. Light bounces from the tops of calm waves as they drift towards the face of the cliff, stroking its cheek then slipping away again like a playful lover.

'Here we are,' says the driver, dark cap pulled low to shield his eyes.

A dark building stands stark against the bright sky, its sharp, pitched rooves like tile-covered blades jutting into the blue.

'Let me out,' he says, yanking at the door handle.

'You agreed to stay in the car, Tobias.'

'Well, I've changed my mind.'

'Wait. Look.'

A procession of children, some with hands on ropes, older ones with hands on guns pointing at the heads of bound adults. More children follow behind, flowing from the large entrance as if from a burst pipe.

'Isn't that the girl from the papers, the one who was taken from a hotel?' says one of the ghosts. 'And her, she's the daughter of one of those rich families from that charity auction.'

'The Wishing Well Gala?' says the driver.

'That's it. Look, there's loads of them. And that guy, he owns one of those internet market things.'

'She's that porn star who owns the oil company. Christ, what's going on? We're going to need a bigger car.'

One child leads them, the foremost rope wrapped around his wrist and clutched in his small, pale hands.

'Oliver?' says Tobias. 'Let me out of this car, right now. That's my son!'

The door clicks and he swings it open, leaping through and running in one swift motion. He wraps the boy in his arms with no concern for the trail of drooling men and women behind him.

'Oliver. I'm so sorry. I never should've let them take you.'

'Don't worry, Dad. I'm fine. I've made some new friends and I've learnt how to tie knots, look.'

He holds out the rope with a look of pure pride on his face. The adults behind shuffle on the gravel drive, faces gaunt and vacant as if starved of their sanity as well as food.

'Well done,' Tobias says, with a rueful smile. 'You'll have to teach me how to do that.'

Four dark spots hover in the corner of his eye. The tears

morph them into people, perched atop the clouds, hooded figures watching, waiting. *For what?*

He wipes away the tears and the figures disappear with them.

Just a trick of the light. Exhaustion.

'Shall we go home?' Tobias asks.

Oliver holds out his hands, spreading his fingers wide. The vacant eyes of the prisoners swell, awareness streaming back in. They try to lift their arms to shield their faces, but the ropes hold them fast. Shouting, screaming, wailing, each and every one of them terrified of an invisible threat. As Oliver clenches his hands into fists, they all fall to the ground, shaking and crying, grazing their skin across the gravel. The children all cheer, the older ones firing rounds into the air, the younger ones hugging each other and spinning around in circles, broad grins on every little face.

'Okay, Dad,' says Oliver. 'We can go now.'

***

ABOUT THE AUTHOR

Jethro Weyman

Jethro is a nineties child born in High Wycombe raised in Hemel Hempstead and has grown into a cycling, bouldering, wandering physiotherapist working for the NHS in Birmingham, England.

He dreams to one day write for a living, and by living he means pay for one grocery shop per month (or two). He believes small goals are the key to the longevity of sanity. Though, as can possibly be told from his work, this is not necessarily working as well as planned.

He enjoys making people think. Even if that thought is, 'What the hell was that all about?' or 'We need to keep an eye on this one.'

He hopes you've enjoyed what he has to say, and if you didn't, he kindly requests that you write your opinions down on a piece of paper, fold it up nice and tight, then hold it just above a flame. He's very perceptive, and smoke signals are his favourite form of communication.

Printed in Poland
by Amazon Fulfillment
Poland Sp. z o.o., Wrocław